D1604093

Humanities), 1970 (c1968). 129p (African writers series) 75-
125671. 1.25 pa.   ISBN 0-435-90053-6

This is the first novel written by a Tanzanian. Palangyo spent some
time at the famous Iowa University writing school, and his book is
much more subtle and skillful than the average African first novel.
It deals with a well worn theme; a young man growing up with his
family and marital problems being intensified by difficulties attending
independence and the early years of African national administration.
But it is an intelligent and mature book. Its pace is slow for it is
highly introspective, a feature rare in African novels to date. But it
has a sensitivity and perception that set it apart from many recent such
books with their mixture of anthropology, biography and melodrama.
An interesting work, not typical of recent novels from Africa. Could
interest a wider readership than those concerned only with Africa.

AFRICAN WRITERS SERIES
Editorial adviser · Chinua Achebe

53

Dying
in the Sun

AFRICAN WRITERS SERIES

Dying
in the Sun

PETER K. PALANGYO

HEINEMANN

LONDON NAIROBI IBADAN

Heinemann Educational Books Ltd
48 Charles Street, London W1
POB 25080 Nairobi · PMB 5205 Ibadan
MELBOURNE   TORONTO   AUCKLAND
HONG KONG SINGAPORE
SBN 435 90053–6
© Peter K. Palangyo 1968
First published 1968
First published in African Writers Series 1969

Printed in Malta
by St Paul's Press Ltd

To G.F.H.

The zig-zag valley that marked the southern end of the village was still at the horizon, and from the slanting shadow that faithfully attempted to caress him, Ntanya estimated the time to be about five o'clock.

Five o'clock, and yet it still so hot and he had seven more miles to go. Ntanya wiped with the torn sleeves of his shirt the round beads of sweat collecting on his face, and in the process a stream strayed into his eyes and mouth; he spat with bitter vehemence as his hands fumbled to untie the knot of the soiled kerchief on his neck to wipe his irritated eyes. He cursed with all his power, cursed the world and life, cursed those fat 'men of the book' in their shiny cars; but most bitterly he cursed God for this world's and his condition as he slumped down with exhaustion on the scorched grass. A sadness verging on despair descended on him, a sadness so harrowing in its sensuality he could not even feel the blood trickling from the wound pierced through his torn trouser seat.

The sun was still biting down with its tropical violence and the dry heat had ebbed but little. Ntanya shied away from the sun in what was now a hazy consciousness that verged on a dream or a nightmare, unaware that the pockets that covered his buttocks had slid off because of the slippery blood. He was unaware of exposing his nakedness. Broken people are alone and therefore have no nakedness.

Ntanya lay there in a condition beyond pain and pleasure only for a while before he came back to himself slightly relieved in the way that a prisoner in great need of urinating feels relieved after he has been allowed to urinate a little. He came back to a feeling of pain in his bottom and a great hunger in his bowels. His throat was scorched so that he could not even swallow. He looked around him and noticed that the cloth bag that carried all he had in the world had been stolen; in it had been the gospel by St. John in Swahili that he never read and valued only because he was given it by his mother, the little change that his former master had thrown him, the wooden comb that he made himself and other such bits and pieces. He noticed that he had been in, well, he did not know in what, for a greater time than he thought because his shadow was now much longer. He looked at the footpath that led to his destination, a path that looked like a long coiled snake whose tail faded in the horizon of the scorched grass. He must get 'home'. His father must not die before seeing him. And yet deep down he knew that he had reached the end of his tether. Some string had snapped in the very centre of his being and he did not quite know how to mend it or whether one should mend broken strings at all.

'There are some people who just don't belong, some people who are marked off from birth and isolated to carry a bigger and bitter cross of suffering,' his wise mother had once told him as she sat crouched on the floor, threshing, and isolating beans that were rotten in the kernel. Ntanya had always known that this vicious malady was in him but had never quite believed it. He remembered how as a little boy he had been bow-legged and clumsy. He had been ugly with a barrel for a head. He had not been quick to learn, and had lacked the grace and agility that were so important if one was to be well thought of by other boys. They had jeered him for his clumsiness and nicknamed him 'clam', 'snail' and 'barrel head'. As a result he had spent a considerable amount of time playing with his sister until she would call him a girl. He remembered so well how ten years before his favourite sister Amina had called him a 'barrel head'. In the intense purity of a child's anger he had thrown a stone at her with such fury that he had broken her leg; from that time on life was never the same. He had gone off and disappeared in the village for three days unable any more to face anything, until he was found by Masina the medicine man, starving and unconscious, with a half-slit neck resulting from an attempted suicide, done with God knows what. It was this scar that he now covered with a kerchief tied round his neck to emulate a tie.

He remembered now the smile of understanding and pardon that played on his sister's face as she lay on the floor of the family hut while her leg was suspended and tied to a pole put there by Masina for this very purpose. He remembered Amina saying in her last words, coming from deep down in her soul like an echo and only partly understandable, 'It is not your fault, my brother, you were just hitting at your ugliness and not me. I was in your way and I am sorry. Please pardon me.' He had gone and crouched beside her terrified and broken. He had put his head on her face and without saying anything, cried as bitterly as a teenage boy, with big round tears dropping down on his big monkey-cheeks. He had cried until his eyes were ember-red. Then there was suddenly a wall between him and his sister. An invisible chasm had developed and he saw her like the valley he had once seen in his dream – pure and inapproachable. His sister was now calm, as the pains had subsided, but there was something terrible and frightening in her calmness. Masina had always said that before death there was a period of calm painlessness, a sort of ultimate relief. Ntanya had then crouched on his knees in an intense religious supplication. One hand had guarded against the swarm of flies that were invading Amina's rotten wound, and the other had dug deep into the earthen floor as though to squeeze, not so much pardon as, understanding from it. He remembered his half-blind grandmother walking in silently, burdened down by her grief and age, he half consciously saw those two broad holes of her nose which had hovered above his sister with a sepulchral expression, big and dilated by the smell they had detected, the smell they knew so well, the terrible smell of death.

C

She had moved close, so rigidly, with a finality that resembled deliberation, and an expression on her blind face that was beyond pity, understanding or pardon. She had moved quietly with the suffering which had been too tediously repeated and which found expression only in the quiet whining deep down in the bowels, like the mute suffering of an animal whose sex has been injured. Quietly she had come close like a bad-good angel and now he remembered, only half consciously, that she had taken him into her lap and rocked him gently to sleep.

He had slept for a long time, only to wake up to a great commotion of neighbours and relatives looking at him with eyes of accusation and pity, for after all he had killed her. There was great sorrow in and outside the family hut with a few of the old women pealing a shrill cry here and there as they envisaged their own too-near dreadful death, on their own family hut's earthen floor. The younger mourners had only sobbed quietly in their souls or simply looked on with mistrust and without understanding, like a flock of sheep which has been driven to an October-dry grassland. Amina's three-year-old curious sister pressed on to the lap of her grandmother, whom she called mother, and asked, 'Mother, how long is Amina going to stay there, is she still asleep?' Her grandmother had simply fondled her and said nothing; not understanding, but being a well-brought-up child, she had said nothing more and had put on a show of sorrow like everybody else.

Ntanya now shaking out of sleep focused his mind's eyes on what had happened, but it was as shapeless as a rainbow mixture of industrial points, punctuated by the individual poignancy of the screams and sobs of the old women. Try as he would, he simply could not shake his mind into a proper kaleidoscope and he could not be roused any more. He had broken like an over-played metal bar on a marimba. He now looked without seeing, listened without hearing. He could only now remember the graveyard scene. He could see a million times a day the image of Amina, wrapped in wet goatskin and

4

lowered into a hole, with only a twig of the plant used for demarcation and fences planted next to her to remind people not to dig there.

These were the memories that occupied Ntanya as he lay on the worn earth, the same kind of earth that ten years before had swallowed Amina. He picked up a handful of soil in his hand, poured it on to the other, and quietly let it trickle through his fingers back to the ground. The sun was now right over near the hills. It was no longer too hot and his thirst was not as painful, though his throat was still dry. He stood up to go and noticed that his joints seemed over-oiled, and that he was swaying a bit in his movements. His shadow was now very long, and looking at it he peeled off an unnatural laugh as he said to himself: 'That is the only faithful companion and friend I have ever had in my life.'

He plodded quietly on like an unwilling animal. Staggering a bit, he ascended the southern hills of the village. He reached the edge of the hills and was looking down into the only beautiful thing he had ever known in his wretched world – the village from the hills. The village minus its people with all their foulness, disease, suffering and constant death. He remembered his mother long ago saying that there would come a day when people will live and be happy and healthy and it would be only the old who would die. He was then too young to understand, and his mother had died in childbirth the following reaping season. He now wished, without much feeling, that this mother had lived to decipher for him now what she had meant.

He climbed the last incline and was faced by the pure beauty-offering of Kachawanga village to the golden light of sunset, much as a little proud and mischievous girl shows off to adults her new kanga. Kachawanga is a remarkable village, set apart in geography as in spirit. Ringed by mountains, there were only two ways of getting into or out of it. From the north the bowl had been opened by the devil for the scourgers of Kachawanga: invading strangers, foul disease-bearing winds

5

and, a long time ago, floods. The way from the south had been opened by God for an escape route from all these afflictions. That is why as common hearsay has it, Maputa, one of the mythological founders of the village, at the moment of being flushed out of Kachawanga by one of those terrible floods, had yelled 'Now, leave the palm of God behind.'

As Ntanya looked down upon the village, his heart seemed to melt inside him. The trees seemed taller and darker in their mystery as they strained to assert themselves before the fading sun, and the smoke of evening supper coyly caressed the receding light on the hillsides. The middle of the bowl was now dark and the orange colour offered itself warily only to the eastern corners of the village. Ntanya breathed hard to fill his strong lungs with the cool village air which smelled, at least in memory, of mashed bananas in groundnut gravy. His heart was beating hard like a man driven into ecstasy by the beauty of a strange woman whom he is not sure whether he should approach or not. Even from where he stood the village started to come to life; for the village was really alive only during the evening while everybody prepared for the death-life of the night. Cattle getting back to the village were starting to moo for their calves and herdboys were yelling goodbye to each other, to keep away the fear of night. Mothers would be busy with their pots trying to fill the bellies of their men, and specks of fire could be seen scattered all across the village. Here and there an owl cried, bringing death to the unfortunate; Ntanya could hear in his mind's ear the subdued sob of the recipient of the message.

Ntanya plodded on slowly and indifferently till he was at the door of his home, then unwillingly he said 'Hodi.' His teenage sister was the first one to hear him and she recognised his voice immediately. She threw down the bunch of bananas she was slicing for the family supper and excitedly ran out, yelling, 'Ntanya is home, Ntanya is home!' There was a great commotion in the household as his two brothers and his other

6

sister scrambled out and, getting stuck at the door of the hut, yelled at each other in fury. 'Welcome home, Ntanya,' they all screamed as they pulled him inside and he obediently and rigidly bent down to get through the four-foot door into the smoky warmth of the hut.

He went on to kneel by the side of his half-deaf, half-blind grandmother, whose mind was also starting to fail. 'My son,' she said, 'come near so that I can feel you.' They touched. 'Your mother doesn't see too well anymore.' Mama Ntanya, as everybody called her, was a mother only in service and dedication to these half-orphans. She was actually their paternal grandmother who had either been too defiant in her health or else in a deep and mysterious way had appeased the spirits enough to live so long. Nobody really knew which was true.

Ntanya crouched between her and the dying embers of the supper fire. Glancing to his side he noticed the diffuse, amorphous shadow he cast on the grass wall, interrupted here and there by his sister and brothers who were standing around as if they were watching in fragile silence the birth of a goat, or an Arab perform his false miracles. Mama Ntanya passed her coarse, bony hand over Ntanya's face, neck and shoulders with the touchy temerity of a child picking up bird eggs or the delicate thoroughness of a doctor examining a dying patient. Then she sighed deep in her being and tears rolled down her ancient face. This sent an electric wave of understanding around the spectators who ceremoniously lowered their heads as if in prayer. 'Is he dead, mother, is father dead?' Ntanya inquired casually about his father.

Word of mouth had come to him in the town, telling him that his father was sick and near death and that he wanted before he died to see his son, bless him, and leave him the affairs of the family. Without understanding or caring, Ntanya had sold his only good pair of trousers to get home. Without understanding or caring he had lost his sixty-shillings-a-month job because his boss would not give him time off to visit his dying father. 'It is not exactly my fault your father is dying,' his boss had said. 'It is either your job, or your presence at your father's death-bed.' And with this his boss had thrown Ntanya's last two shillings at his feet, since he had already spent the rest of the month's salary in advance. Without understanding, he now was asking casually whether his father was dead or not. God, his father! He had never known what the word father meant, now or any other time. He never understood what brought him here. It was not filial piety. That had gone, since filial piety is only a meaningless response, in the way that a child learns to go to the toilet and sticks to the custom once and for all for sixty years. He had come to see a man he had never known, a man who a hundred times had kicked him out while he was hungry and half-naked. This man had caused the death of his mother through unfairly inflicting upon her the corroding sorrow of the spirit. This man's sole claim on him was fatherhood – and he was not even sure of that. His only real claim on him was that he was a fellow sufferer. We suffer together and therefore we are relatives.

'No it is not because of your father I am crying. We, your father and I, belong to the old and we die the old way. We die to relieve ourselves of both the joys and scars of life. Living

8

is very little more than the knitting of a necklace of scars, like this one.' With trembling hands she fondled the dirt-coated bead necklace she had worn since when she was a girl; it was wearing out its twelfth string. 'Like those strangers with a new religion who lately have come to the village and, I hear, count beads with holy words on their lips to forestall misfortunes, everyone accumulates his beads of scars and counts them without any intention of forestalling misfortunes. It gets tedious at times, especially if one has too many beads, and then one wants to stop both fingering the beads and the little, too little intervals between the beads. No, my son, I am weeping for you, for the big beads you have already been given and the ones you have yourself accumulated and the ones you are yet to get.' This half-conscious soliloquy was anxiously interrupted by Onya, his sister. 'You must be hungry and thirsty; I will fetch you something to drink and eat.' She quickly disappeared into the food compartment fenced off by the grass stockade that Ntanya had built a year before. As she went, Mama Ntanya went into an ecstasy of crying, clenching with her fingers deep down into the ground, pleading with all the spirits and gone-by relations to have mercy on Ntanya, explaining as if in court that Ntanya was not fully responsible for his misfortunes. Then the little boys and girls quietly sobbed, with their lips moving in children's silent holy prayers for the grown-ups' problems that they did not understand, pleading for their 'mother' and father and their brothers, but most of all for themselves.

Ntanya was moved to a tenderness of love and sorrow and his lips dropped as tears of indirected tenderness and love ebbed slowly down. His mother was now shaking like a leaf and he crouched down and held her in his arms tenderly, as tenderly as if she would melt or break to pieces. Onya brought a big bowl of sour milk and nudged him in his side. He then felt how dry his throat was. Since his hands were busy his sister held the bowl to his mouth and he swallowed quickly and greedily like the Sahara Desert swallowing the waters of the

9

Nile. Then satisfied, he shook his head with the tenderness of a child that has finished suckling and is therefore going to sleep on the mother's tender breasts. As though the milk came from his mother, he held her closer and tenderly till he could hear the fast beating of the old heart that did not have much longer to go. By now her crying had subsided and she lay there quietly, so many bones in a loose skin with a history and, exhausted, went to sleep. Ntanya got up, quietly and carefully, so as not to wake her from her momentary peace, so as not to bruise her wounds for just a little while. Quietly he laid her on her bedstead after Onya had spread out her cow-skin, the only thing which separated her from the cold and only too-ready-to-receive earth. Obediently like a child – and by now Ntanya's mind was roaming over many ages ago before him when his mother was a little fat baby girl being quietly laid to sleep – she did not wake from this peace, and with her many-holed blanket they covered her to sleep.

Quietly, Ntanya moved to the fire, feeling rather dizzy, the weight of the day on his shoulders. He stirred the dying embers and called his little brother and went on to whisper in his ears things which nobody could hear, electric messages of compliance and understanding that caused a fragile smile to play on his brother's small well-curved lips. They were all around him now, laying their hands on his shoulders and his bent knees, trying to express a sense of solidarity like politicians talking union. They all sat around quietly, without anybody wanting to break the silence with words. Ntanya stretched his long legs across and above the dying fire and a joint snapped noisily. His youngest brother burst out laughing and quickly threw a look at his sister, his mentor of good manners, and in his youthful knowledge he knew that she disapproved, so he immediately stopped and sat down facing the fire in a posture that emulated his brother. Ntanya silently put his arm around his youngest brother and pulled him to his side, and silently they all sat again to wait for the one who would break the silence. They sat on like that till the whole hut was graveyard-silent and the golden flicker in the fire swallowed up in darkness. Slowly the silence swallowed them, one by one, the silence crystallised in the consciousness of the young ones, and one by one they dropped into the darkness of sleep, the youngest hanging his head over his brother's strong and coarse thigh with a limp neck like that of a dead chicken. Finally there was only one consciousness in the hut, Ntanya's; a consciousness that, once diffuse, was starting to crystallise from history, and geography and the future like clouds collecting on the top of Kilimanjaro, that were starting to condense to a point. His body and mind became electrified into acute sensation and clarity. He collected himself and quietly sent them all to bed, each to his assigned area on the cold earth with only banana leaves forestalling the would-be oneness. All the time he was telling himself, 'I'll put them all to bed. God, you can see I'll put them all to bed, quietly and tenderly' as if to reconfirm what deep down he believed in – his innocence.

When he came to Onya who had fallen asleep in an unladylike posture he noticed how pretty she was. He lit a match to examine her closer. At fourteen, she looked like a grown-up woman, with gloss and colour coming in under her chocolate face and a conical breast come to a point as sharp as a pin under her cheap dress. She was strongly built and stout, built to bear many children, for strength and fecundity ran in the family. Ntanya was thinking and swearing to himself as he assessed her beauty with pride, that he'd be there, he'd be there for whosoever married her and if he misused her the way his father had treated his mother – here he clenched his fists and grinned in his unachieved fury – he would kill him. He looked at her again, his eyes proudly caressing the sleeping outlines that were slightly exaggerated by the faint light of the match. Her uncommitted brown was just right, not too white to get freckles and exhibit her feelings, not too dark to be mysterious. His heart beat faster in his chest as he encountered his sister's beauty in its totality. He now understood the story he had once been told that if a man saw God he would die. He had examined her so carefully, like a woman who has just discovered in her nudity before a mirror her infinite beauty, and whose heart is beating peacefully in joyful horror. The unnoticed match burned down to a flicker between his fingers. That hurt. Quickly he threw it down and licked his fingers.

Quietly, he knelt down beside her in the uneasy darkness of the hut. He pushed one arm below her supple neck and the other below the round protruding buttocks. He slowly picked her up, like a soldier picking up a comrade hurt in war, and laid her down on that rough-hewn bedstead which Ntanya had made he didn't remember how long ago. As he laid her down she woke up and put her arms on Ntanya's shoulders, whispering, 'You must be strong for us. You must be strong. You are a man,' and with that she lapsed back to sleep. Ntanya lingered on in the hut a little longer, gazing into the darkness, seeing nothing. Gazing into the darkness of his soul, there was a glimmer of light advertising dawn. The happenings of the day and of the last few hours, and they had been many indeed, were starting to sort themselves out into distinct patches, like a meeting of old men breaking down into age-group committees. His daytime experiences were starting to crystallise into a pattern though it was still rather blurred, and needed further focusing. He must not disturb these crystallisations; one must not disturb the rising of the sun no matter how much of a hurry one is in, one must wait, one must count one's fingers over and over again till the sun rises. Ntanya was going to count his fingers and wait for this silent self-birth of reorganisation in the dark forest of his soul.

How quiet the hut was in its uncanny peacefulness. Once in a while there was the scratch-scratch of the old soul scratching a louse off her dry skin. There was noise of life still stealing through the darkness of the village. Boys and girls playing hide and seek, hyaena and lion, with lighted grass torches. Maybe the noise had been there throughout. Maybe it was only the stillness of the hut that made it more audible.

Ntanya stretched himself out. He noticed a new strength coming into his muscles. In spite of all the walking, he was no longer tired. His dying father was asleep and the orders of the village medicine man were that he was not to be disturbed. All of a sudden, he felt he must see his father, just look at him. He tried to build up his father's image in his mind, and to his surprise he could not. He tried to close his eyes and create his father's physical outlines but again he failed. He moved across the clearing in front of the family hut, slowly across the shrub planted against the white ants into his father's hut which faced west. Quietly, he removed the axe-hewn plank that formed the door of the hut and heard the feeble breathing of his father. He lit a match and hid it in the cup of his hands. He must not wake up the dying man. His father was almost covered with a goatskin, though his face and feet were bare. He moved closer. The old man's mouth was wide open, his hair now brown and collected in little beads like that of a Hottentot, leaving most of the scalp bare. There was something in the old man's helpless posture that raised in Ntanya a mixed feeling of nausea, contempt, hatred and pity. It was not at all like the helplessness of Mama Ntanya. Hers was the helplessness of victory, the helplessness of an impala that has been shot with a rifle and falls down staring at the hunter.

No, the helplessness of the old man was different. Ntanya stared at this dying thing, his father who had so quickly turned into an object of embarrassment. He twitched slightly with revulsion. The once strong, ugly and fierce face had lost all its lustre. The skin was hanging loosely, disgustingly loosely, and the once ugly scar on the left cheek had folded in like a cave. The eyes that were once so bright red with rage or drink, perpetually busy finding someone to be dealt with by physical and psychological violence, had now become sunken as though to hide themselves from this ignominy. Ntanya looked on, emptied of all his bitterness, to this ghost appearance of defeat. He wished his mother could be resurrected just for a moment to witness this, just for a moment. He remembered a long time ago – oh! so long ago – his mother falling to the ground with blood spurting out of her mouth as she slumped under his father's heavy drunken blow. He remembered her saying to her husband, in resignation to her impending dreadful death, that his strength would one day pass. He remembered the day so well though it was long ago. He remembered darkness coming into his soul as he clenched his tiny fists in anger and told himself that one day he would kill his father.

It had been only a few yards from where he was now standing, witnessing his mother's prophecy come true. Only a few years ago, and now here his father lay devoid of his most important manly attribute – strength. Oh how he wished his mother were alive just for a moment to look at the sight of the man she had served so faithfully and who had killed her. And as he stood wishing all this, the sun in his heart rose higher and higher in the sky. The patterns in his soul were becoming clearer. He must not by-pass anything. He must see everything in its glaring clarity. As he was concentrating on the pattern of his life growing in his soul and the true picture of everything slowly becoming cogent, images like water spilt on the ground slowly forming streamlets, his father made a movement. It was a move of desperation, of a man suddenly finding himself in a desert alone. He tried to turn around in his sleep that was not sleep. He tried desperately and helplessly. Ntanya wanted to help him turn. He was still asleep. Ntanya stretched his hands to help him, stretched them until he could almost touch him. Then something happened. He could not move his hands. He could not touch him. He tried, but something seemed to tie him back. There was no bitterness or revenge in his heart any more, but he could not stretch his hands to help him. He was trembling slightly and tears were collecting on his face, but try as he might he could not help his father turn over.

He stood there for a while more, shaking and trembling but unable to move. Finally and abruptly, confused and without understanding, like one walking out of a bad dream, he dashed out quickly and unconsciously. He banged his head badly on the roof of the low hut. He remembered only later, much later, that on his way out as he touched his face he was quietly whispering to himself, 'Ssh, don't wake up my father.' In the open he noticed that the moon had come out, a late and bashful moon that shone as if forced. So far it did not light the western hills of Kachawanga. People were not in the village yet. Children were still lost in their games. Husbands and wives, boys and girls, were quarrelling here and there. They were always quarrelling. He felt it was late, and wondered whether they would stay up all night for fear of the unknown world of sleep. But tomorrow began the second week of the ninth month, and therefore the reaping season would start. They were staying up to celebrate. It was always the same, year after year. One worked to death to plant and then one night, only one night, one harvesting to thank all the spirits that stood by, forestalled evil while one worked. He could not sleep. Not tonight. Something was happening in him, he must see it through awake. In the meanwhile he must occupy himself, so as not to disturb what was going on inside him.

He remembered a childhood friend of his a long time ago, who had gone to school for years in far-away countries. He had heard that he was now back, and stationed in the village as a representative of those men with expensive clothes and houseboys. He must visit him to pass the evening until he was tired. His childhood friend did not live far, just across the valley.

James was a man of the book. Little bits of information, patches scratched by time on the recording sheet of his memory, kept unveiling themselves at some not-so-opportune moments. He would for instance quote an obscure politician's speech without the least provocation to some awed old men as he discussed his village development plans with them. The bag of his mind was filled with hanks of knowledge, some small and large, and once in a while one could shake it, and there would be a terrible rattle. It was at such times that one had a hard time telling whether the smile that played on his face or impish glitter in his big African eyes were one of those little pebbles of knowledge, revealing a brighter side of James himself.

Ntanya knocked three times but there was so much noise inside that nobody could hear. He stopped to find out the nature of this noise. James was authoritatively discussing the new rehabilitation plan. Looking through a crack in the door he saw James seated at his smooth writing table, cluttered with official correspondence files, and the same stamps as the ones he had seen on the writing table of his last employer. He saw James, half-seated, half-standing, so as not to crease his expensive suit, surrounded by half-naked bent old peasants, who looked bored and eager to be given a chance to talk. He could not hear and see at the same time. He had to press either his ears or his eyes close to the crack. Either – or. When it was 'either' he could feel the immobility of the room. The old men were getting impatient, especially the one with an army leftover coat which looked older than the old man himself. This old man was squatting on the cold cement, making an invisible diagram on the floor, partly to occupy himself, partly to keep track of what was going on on his mind and partly to prevent him losing his temper, for the last man who had lost his temper with James, and therefore with the government, had been sent away from the village indefinitely.

When it was 'or', Ntanya could see only a little boy years ago, rather plump with hidden elephant eyes and loose feminine cheeks, playing in the mud alone, because all the other boys despised him. Yes, he could only see this little chubby and dirty boy all of a sudden grown out of proportion and clothed in Scottish tweed, sitting there authoritatively with a government stamp on his desk, telling these ignorant villagers how to improve their own condition.

Ntanya could see the old peasant getting progressively more impatient, as he spat more and more on the floor in spite of disapproving glances from James. The hut was getting too small for what was going on, and James appeared only too prepared or too happy for what was going to happen. Suddenly, snap, the old man crystallised the suspense. Like a machine he stood up shaking his finger in anger at James; his nimbleness was quite surprising. It was difficult to imagine that so much feeling could be enclosed in such a pretence of a human framework. The scene looked almost pathetically funny, like a puppet show. The lean old man with a suffering face shook inside his big leftover army coat like a snake. He was trembling all over, shaking his finger at James. His dehydrated lips were pursed as he attempted to speak, but he could not. Something must have lodged right in his throat. Quickly, like a snake, he spat on the ground and, as if this had cleared his throat, he invoked the name of his grandmother twice, and then started, in a high-pitched voice, words following each other rapidly, if indistinctly. 'I don't understand you nor your breed, nor what is happening to your country. We did not understand the white man, and that was not strange since they were of another tribe. But you,' and this time he pointed at him with less vigour since the lump in his throat was there no more, 'you were born here, you have been suckled with our milk, and today you tell us that the villagers have got to be moved from this land bestowed upon us by our fathers, this land,' he quickly touched the ground that was not ordinary earth but cement, 'this land where our mother and their mothers and our children lie waiting and looking at us. No. One who doesn't have his father's grave to weep at is not a man. Tell your Government that we'll die here — they can find another place to plant their cotton.' By this time all the other old men were standing and their spokesman hung his head in what could be either despair or dejection. Suddenly he opened the door and dashed out, followed by the other peasants with their heads bowed. The leader practically ran over Ntanya but, as they looked one at the other, they recognised their bond and just shook their heads at each other. The old men quietly disappeared into the darkness that was waiting for them, the same darkness which had covered their fathers.

James was still sitting at his expensive table writing notes on a pad, maybe a report to the Government, unconcerned about the old men's presence or absence. Ntanya studied his features. He was big and rather ugly with a roundish belly. His muscles hung loose on his flesh, as they always hang loose on these people with shiny cars and houseboys. Below his left eye, Ntanya could still recognise the scar he had given James when he was a small naked boy playing in the mud.

Ntanya wondered whether or not he should enter or whether he should go home. It is true they had been friends when they were small children playing and crying together, fighting each other. That was long ago and James was not a Government official then and did not have expensive clothes. How was he going to react to this broken peasant in tatters? Ntanya decided to go in. He knocked twice. Without raising his head James snapped, 'Go away. I am going to write to the government and you will see just how powerful the government is.' Ntanya coughed. This time James raised his eyes quickly to look at him and then lowered them back to his files only to realise that this was a different peasant, his playmate of the old days. Without much feeling he extended his arm. Since he was very tall, he appeared as if he was looking down on Ntanya, like one shaking hands with a patient in bed. This was not exactly what Ntanya had expected, even though he did not really know what he had

18

expected. Maybe he did not expect an embrace, but neither did he expect a non-committal, 'Hallo, Ntanya', after so many years. Ntanya's mind was moving very fast, as if it was not occupied already. There were many pictures on the wall including a map of the village with many coloured pins on it. Maybe the room was not exactly luxurious, but Ntanya was surprised by the number of books, some eaten by insects and all laden with dust. Ntanya riveted his eyes on his host again. A carefully measured smile was playing on James's face making his scar look like a hole. 'Sit down. How have you been?' Ntanya did not know what to say; again he remembered the fat little boys playing in the mud. The voice echoed back in his mind – sit down, sit down, sit down – like a noise across the valley of Wachita. Somehow he felt it was grossly unfair. He had not expected an embrace, but it was unfair all the same. They had once touched each other a long time ago. It had not been like this; he had not shaken a hand that was soft and slimy, almost like the breast of a dirty woman. Then Ntanya felt that maybe he was wrong. Maybe there was no connection at all between this government official with official stamps on his desk and the boy who had played with him. Why should there be? After all, he could not exactly ask him to go and play naked in the rain with him now. No, things were different, just as after waking up from a dream. He was extremely embarrassed, but he only knit his hands and sat down mumbling slowly, as if to address himself, that he was not dead yet and so he guessed he was doing all right. Without much feeling they exchanged a few pleasantries, such as their whereabouts during the past ten years. They were talking in quiet voices, failing to hide the fact that one was talking because he had taken the liberty of entering this room with a government official in it and the other was simply diagnosing another unproductive hand in the village. They all had the same story, James was thinking, as he half-listened and half-read a news-paper. There was always bad luck, or God had not wanted them to succeed, and they always ended by talking about death, about how everybody was going to die anyway; they thought of themselves going to rest from tribulation but other people were going to die. When Ntanya mentioned death, James turned his head up as if somebody had pricked his fat stomach with a needle. The last peasant who had come to him begging for food for his starving children had been turned away because he had been reported lazy. He had ended by talking about death. On the following day James had found him hanging from the baobab tree in front of his house staring at him, dead. The two men stared at each other for some time the way people should. For a split second they touched again almost as if they were just the little boys rolling over and over in the mud, laughing.

Then Ntanya started talking while looking at his friend. 'I need a friend, James. All my other friends are either dead or working as houseboys in faraway places. I need a friend badly, like when you were afraid a long time ago in the darkness and I held your hand home. So much is happening to me, I am almost feeling dizzy in my heart. I need somebody to hold on to. My father is dying. You know I don't like him but he is my father and he is dying. He is not powerful any more, he cannot beat me up now. He is just lying in bed, looking without seeing, moving his lips without speaking. I need somebody to stand by at his grave. Please help me.' With this he hung his head.

James felt relieved. Ntanya was not going to commit suicide after all. It was just his poor father who was going to die. 'Surely I'll stand by you. Surely, anything you want, Baranya' – he called him their childhood nickname – 'anything; I'm sorry you've had to go through so much. We all have to, don't we? Always somebody dying, always the fear of our own death. My mother is going to die soon too. We with jobs bury our minds in them, but you always face death and as a result you are not afraid. We bury our fear in these files' – he flung the files on the floor – 'and these big houses, and drink, and yelling at houseboys. But deep down in the darkness when we are alone we are afraid of death, just as I was afraid in the darkness that day long ago walking with you, Baranya.' At the end of this speech, which was addressed more to himself then to anybody else, James thrust his hand out and shook Baranya's with the other, embracing him on the shoulder. This time his hand was soft but not slimy; the government official had suddenly turned into a man. They stood there facing each other and warmly shaking hands for some time, the government officer and the broken peasant.

Then Ntanya pulled his arm away. Something was happening in his stomach, a mild nausea, maybe he was going to be sick right there on the cement floor. 'I must go now James, I must go.' And with that he went out.

'I'll walk with you home,' James quietly followed him out into the darkness. Out there in the dark he did not feel as if he was going to be sick any more. He did not know what had stirred his stomach. Maybe it was the picture on the wall, or the worn-out government stamp, or the quick metamorphosis of the government officer. Whatever it was, he had felt dizzy inside there, but now in the darkness that surrounded them his stomach stopped churning. They walked on quietly without exchanging a word. Quietly the two men walked further. It was not at all the same as when they had walked in the darkness long ago when they were children. Then they had laughed and held hands; they had been afraid of the unknown, hidden in the dark. Now they were no longer afraid of the unknown in the surrounding darkness, they were frightened of the known-unknown darkness that had settled on their hearts, and in which they were so far apart. From the same starting point, they were now so separated. Long ago when they were little boys they used to keep calling to each other as they parted with the goats each to his home in the dusk, calling repeatedly across the valley. As they had separated further and further, in spite of their more and more shrill voices it had been difficult to hear each other until they could only hear a faint echo across the valley at which they had each concluded to themselves 'Goodbye Baranya, Goodbye Baranya.' It is true there was still a man in both of them but they were not talking to each other any more. They were each giving a commentary on their experiences which were so vastly different. Ntanya wondered whether the man in the government official would have been revealed, whether he would have embraced and shaken him with hands that were no longer slimy, if they did not have only this one bond – they both had parents they did not like, who were dying like the echo across Mampala valley. In the darkness Ntanya saw the cactus edge that marked his father's banana shamba. As if to conclude his thoughts he said 'Goodbye Baranya.' James replied, 'Goodbye Baranya' and they parted.

When he got up in the morning the sun was already filtering through the grass thatch of the hut. He felt limp as if he had been beaten up. He stretched himself carefully as he felt his sore ribs; the grass on his bedstead was getting thin and his ribs had come into contact with the coarseness of the wooden platform. He thought that his mother must be getting old, old enough to forget to put new grass on his bedstead. She had always done that when he came home announced. Or maybe . . . No!

His eyes looked at the three stones which made the hearth. He gave a careful smile as he saw the little soot-coated pot covered with a dirty black tin plate. His banana porridge breakfast! 'The poor old soul, the poor beautiful old soul,' he said in tenderness and love for his mother. She had always done that. She had groped in the darkness of dawn and her near-blindness to make the children breakfast before they got up. It was always pounded green bananas with a little groundnut oil and water but then that was more than she had. Ntanya cautiously got up. As he thrust his eyes through the small hut door, the opening into the world, he noticed his mother seated in the world cross-legged on the ground with a piece of calico tied round her waist and her other piece of calico (that was all her wardrobe) rippled in a mass on her lap. She was stretching her arms in a yawn which expressed either boredom or impatience with the lukewarm sun. She never had enough sun, never.

Noticing the emaciated body, now bent over cracking fat lice between bloody nails he started with a jerk. 'My God, my God,' he whispered. 'Good morning mother of people,' he said standing by her.

She started a little as she hurriedly rubbed the blood off some of her nails clumsily and imperfectly, and tried to cover the bosom that had once nourished Ntanya's father. Covering her bosom in the sun while bursting lice between her fingers – women! 'Good morning' she said, with a girlish shyness. She was always a woman of few words, she once said that one must learn to suffer quietly. 'Have you eaten your breakfast?' she asked.

'No,' he replied.

She seemed rather hurt. 'I saved the goat Miranda's milk for the last three days for you, you know.'

Not feeling particularly honoured, he slowly replied, 'Thank you mother.'

She resumed her lice bursting. There was an awkward silence. Ntanya was examining her. He was frightened by how ugly she looked, how anciently inhuman the skin that hung loose on the bones. Her bright eyes sunk in, maybe to come closer to the brain to preserve the little sight that she had left, though things were blurred enough as they were. Her head was always shaved. She said she shaved to mourn her dead ones, but Onya

23

had once joked that she only shaved so that she could get more sun. It was never warm enough for her. She had not thought it a joke. Ntanya knelt down beside her and helped her track the fleeing lice. It made him nervous to see her hands shaking as they followed a louse that would invariably disappear into the dirt-brown of the seam. Ntanya was thinking that he'd boil up that calico for her that morning, but he remembered that she had nothing else to put on while the calico was boiling. He also remembered that she had once refused to have the lice destroyed, since they occupied her.

To avoid this, the obvious scrutiny that was going on, she broke the silence. 'You should have seen your father yesterday,' she said non-committally.

'I did but he was asleep.'

'Yes, he said you walked in and jumped out like one going in and out of the lavatory.'

'He was asleep,' he reiterated.

'He has not been good to you or me or to himself. Some strange spirit caught him. I've seen him cry, in between his drunkenness, trying desperately to wrench this strange weight off his soul. He is a sad unfortunate child and he is only hitting at this, this thing in him, when he drinks and becomes cruel. The day he killed your mother.' Ntanya closed his eyes as this horrible scene re-enacted itself in his mind. 'He had told me with sweat on his brows that something heavy had stood on his chest the night before, so heavy that he couldn't breath, my son.' Her bony fingers were on his strong thighs as she pulled him down to sit next to her, and then she went on whispering to him as if to tell the ultimate secret of her life in short whispers of pain so that not even God might hear. 'My son,' she repeated in pain, 'by the time you are as old as I am,' here she spat blessings in the rising sun, 'you will understand and forgive and may take life less seriously. Your father is my son, I carried him here.' She touched her now emaciated womb. 'During hard times; for nine months I expected a lot from him as a reward to himself. He was born in starvation, you know. I tried very hard, very hard indeed. I would go to caves over there.' She pointed at the far hills of Kachawanga that were unconsciously streaked with this sad history. 'I would look for honey for him which I would hide from his starving irritated father – you know how you men get irritable when hungry, Sabulaki!' She evoked the name of her grandfather, the one she had never known. 'How I was bitten by the bees. I thought I would die. And your grandfather just smiled at "my stupidity". Then he grew up, the hunger ended, and I fed him so well after that. I had such white teeth too. I fed him from the mouth till he was four – he was my only son you know. He grew to be a fat boy almost smooth like a girl. I remember his father saying,' she spat blessings into the ground, 'saying that he would never turn into a man because he was so fat. When his father died – I said that God always beats you and wipes the tears – he had left me another man, another husband and at the burial place I wept tears from the eyes only as they laid him to rest. He became a young man and I looked so carefully for a girl for him. I scoured all the village till I met your mother.' There she broke into tears that would only wet her eyes. Her tears must be dried up. 'She, Sabulaki preserve her, was such a beautiful wench, healthy and happy as if she never ate anything but fat and honey. I married them, and then you and the others came and then he, he . . . .' She broke down into a shaking sob, but still no tears came. She lay down her face to the earth as though to hide herself from the now warm sun. Ntanya came closer to her, trying to hold her as he had the night before, but she pushed him away. 'No, we must learn to suffer alone. Go see your father now. If you let him down now you too will die in the field, alone in the sun, with your mouth open. Go see him. At death one needs someone to hold one's hand, a sort of last bond; go see him now the spirit has left him, go see the remains. Get out of my sun!' Ntanya felt sick in his stomach, though his breakfast was still sitting at the hearth. He always felt sick and dizzy at moments like this that brought such clarity to his soul.

Again, the images in his soul were becoming clearer and clearer, the fog was crystallising, as he shut his eyes to close off the rising sun. Ntanya, supposed son of Ruata Bendera, was a man standing on a last precipice. He was going to fall. He could see the abyss opening in the earth below; his father was going to die and his grandmother and his sisters were not going to.

His father was going to die. He could see in his mind the old man stare at the flies that he could not chase away. Ntanya sat there in the shade of the hut, sweating, and he Ntanya Ruata ... Well he must go to see him. Without opening his eyes he moved mechanically into the hut. His father was lying down just like the night before, with small beads of sweat scattered over his face, marks of inert suffering. Ntanya sat himself down on the bedstead. It creaked as if it would fall and the noise woke up his father. His father carefully and painfully rolled over to face his son. The sunken eyes tried to focus on Ntanya; they were still amazingly bright and fresh looking, for even eyes of dead people look bright and healthy looking. There was a moment of mutual embarrassment and guilt as the two men encountered each other. Shakingly the old man closed his eyes and extended his arm. In a moment of moving bitterness Ntanya extended his too, and the hands interlocked like a chain link in darkness. His father had extended his first, and he was going to die. The old man's dry lips were moving but no words came out. One could see that he was trying but all his attempts only increased the beads of sweat on his face. Open mouthed, Ntanya leaned over closer to his father and listened to the broken bits of noise coming from the old man. All he could hear was a repeated monotone 'My my, my . . .' while the old man made the handshake firmer and firmer. Both hands were now wet with sweat. Finally the old man opened his eyes and looked at his son pleadingly like a

26

hungry kitten and then withdrew his hand and slowly rolled over to face the wall.

'My father, my father,' the words rolled out of Ntanya incoherently. The old man had gone back to sleep.

As Ntanya turned he saw his grandmother withdrawing slowly from the hut entrance with her hand over her mouth. She had been watching them, with her unseeing eyes. Ntanya turned around and threw another look at his sleeping father and then walked out. First he walked around the hut unseen and unseeing and then, like a crooked tangent, unconsciously gave himself the illusion of movement from this parabola. He moved straight on between the daze of the noon sun and the chill in his soul. He could not hear the cracked voice of his grandmother yelling 'Where are you going?' as she followed behind, bent and supporting herself on her stave. She had followed him up to the white-ant hedge and drooped in the dust alone. Ntanya did not see her; he had gone on and on without the intention of going anywhere in particular, and repeated loudly to himself 'My my, my . . .'

His father was going to die and all he could say was 'My my, my,' when for the first time they had sat there, the two of them alone, shaking hands and sweating. There had been so much to say, so much to find out and understand when Ntanya had entered the hut; the open grass-land in his soul which was now dust had again reappeared. Now he understood that he had almost seen the lines of his father's history forming in the dust of this ethereal ground and leading into his own lines. He could see it – the whole wiped clean as a farmer cleans his farm to allow millet alone to grow. The whole world had become a stage for him and his father with only a few lines and circles touching his father's and therefore his own lines of history. The whole world had become complementary to the two of them, and at the moment when they had been shaking hands he had been an eager expectant mother waiting for delivery of her first child. He would now discover the cracks in the lines of his father the crack that had put his own lines out of focus and blurred them beyond proportion. It was at this point that his father had only yielded more beads of sweat and, like an aborting mother he had only said 'My my, my . . .' Dying people should not say 'My' but his father had said 'My.' It could have been my son, my dead wife, my death. It could even have been my foot. People are always talking about my head, my eyes, and even my soul and then one is left to wonder what the 'Me' is.

Ntanya noticed that he was standing beneath the big baobab tree which, he had been told when he was a child, had been a twig used to mark the grave of his founding grandfather long, long ago. He did not know how or why he got there. He only remembered that as a little boy long ago he had once hidden himself there when Amina died and that his mother had then told him that, as his grandfather of long ago had been buried there, it was a holy place.

He sat underneath the tree with his head bowed between his thighs, one hand covering his eyes and the other outstretched as if to receive something. A feeble echo was resounding across the valley of his being. 'I have accepted my curse. That is easy enough. I have gone around the world like a lame ostrich picking seeds on a dry brushland. The seeds that I have picked have been bitter at the kernel, but I have limped on quietly and alone with only the grave knowledge of my curse and a hope. A hope of one day understanding the cause of my lameness and what made my brushland dry. My father's father.' Here he held the baobab tree and clutched on to a fragment of the tree's bark with his eyes shut. 'My mother, my God, and all that there is above me. It is hard enough to be cursed but it is a sad child that has been beaten without being told his offence. Mother, you once told me before you went beyond where tears don't reach and eyes don't see, you once told me that God does not beat one and leave him that way. That he comes back to wipe his tears. I have been beaten and I have not complained, I am only asking God to wipe away my tears. I want to understand my sin. Please don't let my father come before I know.'

He had been speaking the last part of his entreaty out aloud as if his host of the other world were there, and all of a sudden he raised his head to heaven as an ostrich does when frightened. Sitting there staring at the sky above he seemed to expect the heavens to crack in the way that the people who had just come to the village were saying that it once did to proclaim one of their leaders a son of God. The heavens had cracked for Jesus. Ntanya sat there looking as if he expected the heavens to crack for him too. It did not crack for him. He looked at the base of the baobab tree but his ancestors did not come up. Scarcely a leaf moved. There was only mocking silence and heat around him. Once in a while a dry leaf cracked in the sun here and there.

He looked about himself again and again. It was a sultry afternoon and even the air felt tired and lethargic. He could see, down below, cattle weighed down with long horns resting in the shade of trees in little multicolour dots. With them little herd boys, either beaten by the heat or half-starved, or both, slept by the cattle. One of the boys had a piece of calico cloth round his waist, its newness indicated by a white spot. He remembered his own herding days and their great hunger. How one was nothing more or less than a consciousness surrounding an empty stomach, and the immense pleasure he had got when his mother had sold enough bananas to buy him a two-shilling piece of white calico.

Maybe his curse had started there. Because he had not had enough to eat, he had been cursed. But this possibly could not be, since he had not refused food. One should not be punished because of a punishment.

He started to descend the hill towards home as he remembered his breakfast sitting by the hearth. A little way see, down below, cattle weighed down with long horns, resting then through the corner of a thicket came Mugia Mabeba, an old friend of his, and a woman in a straw hat and pointed shoes, who therefore could not be from Kachawanga. Mugia wore an old torn fez and his shirt had many holes burnt in it. He had no shoes, and his big feet and his stoop made him look like a large duck. His appearance indicated a reckless life; he had many scars on his face and he walked with a slight limp. His knee caps wanted to come out through the hole they had created in his pants. He must have knelt a lot, praying or begging.

Seeing Ntanya he uttered a few words of surprise, swallowed in a child laugh which echoed and continued in his woman companion. He was a humorous fellow. 'I thought you were dead, man' he said good-naturedly, all the time laughing as they shook hands.

'I would have informed you' Ntanya said without thinking and wearing a forced smile.

Mugia laughed louder and louder, shaking all over and exposing his big white teeth which sprouted irregularly from purple gums. He suddenly stopped laughing and looked sideways at the woman accompanying him. 'This is my woman for tonight' Mugia said, while his eyes rested on the woman. 'I don't even know her name.' He burst out into a laugh again. Ntanya surveyed the woman from her toes till their eyes met; they were the only desirable things. Big brown child's eyes, that looked as if they were pleading for the rest of her. She looked as if she was in a lethargic dream, or walking out of one and tired of it. He forced a smile at her and bowed his head, as though he did not see the dirty arm she was extending. He went on looking at her, as her cry-smile concentrated on Mugia, whose laughter had threatened to go on for ever. She had extremely large breasts that made her whole body appear merely as their extension. Her lower jaw protruded and pulled tight the skin on her face, making one fear that a crack would occur on it if she smiled any farther. Her legs were so thin that there was hardly enough meat to clothe her bones and this made her pointed shoes look terribly oversize.

Mugia stopped laughing and rubbed his tears with the scarred back of his hand, and they both concentrated on Ntanya. 'What's the matter?' they asked in unrehearsed chorus.

'Nothing, nothing at all.'

'Then let's go to my woman's place; she says she's renting a house near the holy tree of your fathers.' Ntanya started. 'I've got some money. Let me see,' he fumbled in his protruding pockets and fished out a ten shilling note. 'It's enough drink and food for us today. My woman will get you a woman too. Right, my woman!' Mugia did not hear the feeble 'yes' from his woman – he was swallowed in his chorus of a laugh again. 'We have the time today, man, and you will deserve it. I thought you were dead,' he said, as he practically knocked Ntanya off his feet with a pat on the shoulder. Mugia suddenly stopped and assumed an air of grave seriousness. He looked Ntanya right in the eyes and put his arms on his shoulder saying 'What really is the matter my friend? Did somebody die?' He ordered the woman to leave them alone for a while; certain things must be faced by men alone.

'No, no, there is no need for her to leave, Mugia. There is nothing wrong, nobody has died in our family for a long time.' Mugia put his arms around his woman's waist or middle, for she had no waist at all, and his other on Ntanya's waist and they started moving. Ntanya could not make up his mind between going to the brothel with this walking laugh and explaining what could not be understood; but walking laugh had his arm on his waist and he just followed on.

The house rented by Maria, for that turned out to be Mugia's woman's name or nickname, was a beer shop which had been converted to a more attractive use, thanks to her ingenuity. It was a bungalow on the western end of Kachawanga hiding itself beneath a tree a few steps from the dust road. It was a sort of crossroad where people had the luxury of doing incognito all those things they should not do. Mugia must have been doing

31

well, because the grass roof had been replaced by a corrugated iron roof without a ceiling and the floor was half cemented. Straw partitions had been made in the east and west ends of the building. To the west each partition had a rough wooden framework straw bed and to the east the rooms were empty save for a few stools and chairs. The middle was a lounge where one could drink while making negotiations.

Silence reigned immediately when the three entered. The occupants who had been talking quietly or just staring at the floor raised their expectant eyes to Maria and she, like a mother-bird come back to the roost with food in its beak, went about shaking hands with everyone and dishing out her cracking smile all round the room, generously to the men and forcedly to the women, like a gentle priest dispensing grace. Ntanya was standing by the door with one hand on his face to shut off the afternoon sun, gazing unenthusiastically at Maria's many and varied chicks. His interest was attracted by an old man sitting in the corner with his sweating feet, one with only three toes, turned into a calabash stand; on his lap sat a young distinctly handsome girl of barely sixteen years. The old man was rather dehydrated with a baldness, leaning to the left, that he perpetually scratched. Maybe it was the scratching that made it bald to start with. Ntanya noticed that he held the girl very close to himself when it was his turn to shake hands with Maria and that instead of shaking Maria's hand he had only pleadingly looked into the cat eyes of the suffocating girl on his lap. He must have been sinking; maybe he had been sinking all his life.

When Mugia saw that Ntanya was concentrating on the old man he moved close to his ears and with subdued laughter whispered about him to Ntanya. Nobody knew who he was, or where he came from. Rumours had it that he once was a son of a chief in some far-off village to the south; that he was once prosperous both in wealth, children and the possibilities of becoming a chief. Then his elder son had turned into a government official and started campaigning against the existence of chiefs. Hearing this, his greying father, feeling his power undermined by his own house, had walked out one night and disappeared. The curse had fallen on this old man's house; his cattle started dying and he took to drinking. First he made his own millet beer and drank at home, until he got tired of his wife weeping by his feet and his children standing there with open mouths. He then went out to the drinking shops, selling little sandwiches of his land. One day he came home and found his house in flames with all his children and his wife dancing around in anguish and agitation. It is said he then looked at his wife and started walking up north while his wife danced her way south. At the end he had reached this house of ambiguities and thanks to the goodness of Maria's heart had stayed on as a grandfather to the whole establishment. One day he had seen this young girl, and they had immediately taken to each other. He had found in her both his daughter and an object of atonement from his curse; she had found protection. Besides protecting her from the whims of Maria and the abuse of the men, he did all the work for her; he even mended her calico and removed the jiggers from her pretty feet, though neither of them knew the name of the other, and they hardly spoke to each other except by questions like, 'My darling, are you hungry?' Or, 'Shall I bring you some beer?' To which the answer was invariably, 'No, father.' At the conclusion of this sad tale Ntanya shook his head in sympathy. Touched and serious, Mugia said that another rumour had it that this old man had once been a regular Don Juan, playing messenger and a handy help in all jobs that required agile musculinity, like tying maize bunches on a tree or helping bleed cattle in the day. He had in this way touched the very bottom of women's hearts, who would willingly open the door when he tapped at an agreed time. When he had grown old he had been ridiculed by the young women who had found young lovers, and he had been considered a buffoon by the older women with whom he had played Don Juan; they would call him an impotent, sonless idiot to his face. In his desperation, he had finished up in Maria's fold and spread his tentacles around this young girl as a sort of historical mirror of his life, giving witness to himself and the public that he had not always been like this. Like an old man polishing and caressing a spear he had used during his successful youthful warrior days, this old man spoiled and doted on the young girl, wetting his mouth in desire that was now calcified once and for all in his mind; he claimed complete monopoly of the girl, and strangely she in turn clung to him like a crab clinging to a dead shell.

Before Mugia finished telling Ntanya this rumour, Maria interrupted from the western partition. She was yelling at the top of her voice. 'I said before there will be no doing these things in the day. There just won't!' You are not animals, dogs, you are still human beings. If you are not, I declare that you are.' A young man walked up, looking down as he tied his waist-cloth. The sitting room roared with laughter, led by the walking laugh; even the young man laughed as he disappeared out to the dusty road.

The old man with the girl on his lap also laughed exposing a bare purple lower gum and two chisel-like brown teeth on the upper. 'They are too warm-blooded, the young men of today,' he stammered. Nobody noticed this remark. All the eyes were set on Maria who came down the aisle pushing a middle-aged woman in front of her, both of them laughing. She stood her by Ntanya and announced that she was going to be Ntanya's woman for the night. Everybody laughed. Ntanya started and moved a little further, probably to get away from the smell.

Maria announced a free calabash for everybody, to celebrate the fact that she was still alive. 'May you live as long as Kachawanga.' The old man, who had all the time been squatted on the floor staring at his toes said, and all but Ntanya responded, 'Yes, may you do so.' This time Maria laughed out aloud, probably the loudest laugh of her life stretching the skin on her face saying, 'Who the hell wants to live long?'

The old man with the young girl said, 'I do.' The crowd laughed again partly at the comment and partly because the middle-aged woman, Ntanya's woman, had now seated a frothing pot of fresh millet beer on the floor and was dishing out calabashes, first to the older people.

'Music, music,' Mugia yelled. The young girl on the old man's lap took herself slowly and gracefully from the clutches of the vein-protruding tentacles and, after casting a pleading look at her grandfather lover, moved as gracefully as a a cat to a black box which stood on a wooden slab; which had previously been used for washing because it was marked with white streaks of soap. She must have been the music mistress and a competent one at that. She opened the box, which turned out to be a gramophone, took off the handle and stuck it into a dirt brown hole on the outside. With infinite care she wound this handle until it would move no more. After changing the needle, she examined the meagre collection of records, five in all, that she must have known by heart since she could not, at any rate, read English.

She threw a look at the customers and clients to see whether anybody had a particular choice, but nobody was paying attention. They had broken down into committees drinking leisurely, with most of the full calabashes sitting frothing on the floor while one calabash passed to and fro within each group. They were all talking in subdued tones or merely nodding assent to the small talk that always accompanies such occasions. Only Ntanya still stood at the door with his calabash in his hands gazing at the setting sun that was not too far from its night home in the western mountains.

Ba ba bu ba Ba ba baba ba bu ba.

The music started roaring. There was a crack on the record which for some reason came up around the 'bu' making it sound like a groaning 'bo-oh'. The little girl stood by the gramophone just in case of difficulty. All the talking stopped as soon as the

35

music started. The calabashes were emptying quickly and Mugia whispered to the middle-aged woman an order for a round for everybody.

The older folks were nodding in tempo with the broken American rhythm while the words were not understood, which was all the better. The gramophone groaned on:

Sitting, sitting, waiting all night for the phone to ring.
My darling where could you be, at the dairy green with Millie?
At the drive-in with Connie or maybe just singing with Rose Ann?
Ba ba bu ba Ba ba ba ba ba bu Ba.

The younger folks moved their waists rhythmically and twisted their shoulders in a controlled yet vigorous fashion. Mugia was now on his third calabash and his movements were evidently influenced by the two previous ones. He was now swaying with taut muscles unaware of the beer that was spilling on to his exposed knee cap from the tilted whirling container. Attention was now centred on him. Even Ntanya gave a weary smile.

Mugia seemed to be the origin of a wave that rippled through everyone except Ntanya and the little girl, producing identical though reduced rhythmic shakes and swaying.

Ba ba bu Baa Ba ba ba Ba ba Bu baa.

Dust was slowly rising from the earthen floor as the taps became more and more uncontrolled. It looked like golden dust in the flecks of light that came through the door and the many rods of light that came through the perforations in the corrugated-iron roof and the mud wall. Except for Ntanya who was determined to miss nothing, nobody noticed the little bits of dust carrying on their own vigorous dance in the light before falling exhausted into the foaming calabashes. Nobody even noticed them in the calabashes and, as our old-man-lover gulped down his beer with a grin, Ntanya was repeating in his mind, 'From dust unto dust . . . from dust unto dust.' Mugia's movements were now turning into an agitated frenzy. With his eyes shut and sweat collecting on his face he was now wriggling vigorously like a top, tapping his big bare feet and clenching and opening his hands in rhythm. It might be added that the people of Kachawanga believed that everybody has got a snake, a sort of pith of life, at the anatomical centre of his body. It could have been that Mugia's pith was wriggling itself silly in all its liquid tensility. Everybody was by now either tapping his feet on the ground or clapping.

Suddenly the music came to an end with an unnecessarily pleading, 'My darling Sue'. There was much applause for Mugia, which he did not appear to mind. He seemed to be a man of rhythmic violence. From his trance of dance he moved into one of laughter and both had the innocence of an animal's act. Like an animal he never laughed for anybody else but for himself, and for the simplicity of his being. He was evidently simple. But as he had commented once, 'What would I do with intelligence here other than rot my gut and commit suicide?' Indeed what does anybody want intelligence for in a thoroughly unintelligent, even unintelligible world? Who needs intelligence when one is chopping wood all day to light a fire for washing somebody else's laundry, or walking, just walking miles looking for work and all you see are big black fat faces in shining cars that blow dust in your eyes so that you cannot see the signs all over the road, 'No work! No work!' which you cannot read in any case? No, Mugia had been insulated by his lucky star. He laughed and danced and made love violently and when he was hungry because he had lost his job or tipped his woman too much, he would cry with the same simple violence until he would cry no more. Then he would laugh because a particular fly was in an embarrassing posture, or the moon looked as if it was falling.

'Music, music,' Mugia yelled as he took another gulp from his fourth calabash.

Ntanya was now seated on the threshold of the door with the old man's girl leaning on his lap holding the calabash for him. He had not finished his calabash, but he was certainly in a good mood now. The young girl had introduced herself as Teresa. Strange, for nobody else had known her name, not even the old man, for whom the excitement had been too much and who was now quietly sleeping in the corner with an open mouth, unperturbed by all the noise. Something had attracted her in Ntanya, something both sensual and deeper. Maybe it was his eyes constantly surveying the room with an understanding, almost vicarious suffering. It could have been the apparent, too apparent explosiveness of Ntanya's silence, like an egg that is about to break into an unknown chick. Women, especially young women, have got a weakness for the surprise of the unexpected. Whatever it was Teresa had taken a surprised fancy to Ntanya and she did not hide it. Maybe that was what made the old man go to sleep with his mouth open.

'Music, music,' Mugia yelled again as he put down his empty calabash, looking at the empty lap of the sleeping old man and turning around to look at Teresa leaning on the lap of Ntanya affectionately unaware of her role. He winked at Maria.

'Let them alone,' Maria was thinking as she moved to put on a new record. 'Let them alone, it's soon going to be dark. They're both troubled children, they deserve the illusion of relief.'

'Oh it's Masengwa,' Mugia said with delight, for he loved his local rolling guitar strummer with his scintillating rhythm. As soon as Mugia had spoken the customers cleared room.

Masengwa turned on something in Mugia and he was already kicking the air like a horse that has been tied to a tree. Without being solicited Maria came up to Mugia to dance. She was used to this. Whenever men started getting drunk they always wanted their women nearby to dance with them even though they finished up dancing alone in the darkness of their drunken ecstasies. Waving, twisting and shaking all in one, alone with closed eyes and sweat all over, around their women, around their reference points. Mugia danced on and on with his arms outstretched, his shoulders and his head pulsating and his waist twisting with the vigour of a bee. Around and around Maria he went, unaware of her with his closed eyes, once in a while touching her, but still unaware of her. Faithfully Maria danced around him, first mechanically and then with her closed eyes she seemed to melt into the pure motion of a liquid, a stream. Like a queen bee she danced around the king unaware of twisting and writhing her waistless middle, swaying her big breasts and extending her arms, extending and withdrawing her arms rhythmically, extending them but without touching her king, only feeling the pulsating waves in the air. Two streams dancing around each other, throbbing in pure motion that seemed to originate from every cell in their bodies. Masengwa seemed to have played this particular piece just for Mugia and Maria, for this occasion, this point in history. For they too were troubled children, they too could make use of the illusion of relief. Masengwa accompanied the dancers with a rising and rising wealth of rhythm, and his droning broken voice wailed into higher and higher levels of ecstasy till the two dancers were like a taut stretched bow. Every nook, every part of their bodies raised its offering into the completeness of this sensual symphony. Masengwa demanded all; he was still beckoning them to higher levels of movement, higher pitches, and they followed on obediently higher and higher, even higher than Masengwa demanded, higher towards the hill, towards the climax of this symphony.

All the customers and clients were now sitting by the walls, some with closed eyes shaking or tapping, all unaware of the calabashes they held slanted, unconsciously pouring their offerings on the ground and on their pants, gowns, kangas and even their half exposed bodies. Ntanya still leaned on the door frame with one arm around the waist of Teresa, and the other one

39

holding the calabash. Nothing had excited him for a long time now. He had been walking along like a cursed demon, unaware of his body and only obsessed by his curse or his imagined curse, by the death of his father. Now here, a jobless, homeless, kinless orphan was dancing in pure abandon unaware of the world, unaware of everything but this dance. Unconcerned even about what he would eat on the morrow when his ten shillings was finished – or maybe it was finished already. Ntanya stood with his mouth open nodding in rhythm with the dancers, tapping his big bare foot on the floor just like everybody else. He was gazing at the dancers without really seeing them. He could not even notice the indescribable calm on Maria's face. Everybody in the room was sweating but Maria's face always seemed to be insulated especially when she was not smiling or laughing, insulated from the extremities of pain or pleasure. It was a face that had seen much suffering that it neither recognised nor registered, maybe because it refused to or maybe it was incapable of distinguishing sorrow from joy. Her whole personality seemed to show this revolt, this rejection of regrouping, categorising experience into pain or pleasure.

Her face was as calm as a mummy or dead person. It had the frightening immobility of death and it seemed completely divorced from the palpitating flesh that danced round and round Mugia. It was only on her arms and her now bare feet that sweat-clusters of muddy dust absorbed her sweat.

Suddenly Masengwa decided to stop. All too suddenly for, as after an earthquake, though his fingers had stopped moving the steel strings, the tremors went on and the echo of the rhythm resounded across the valley of the land of the self-abandon that was no longer aware of Masengwa anyway. Maria and Mugia went on dancing and the spectators went on nodding and tapping, here and there softly clapping. However dancing without music is like a burning fire that is not reinforced with fuel. It slowly died out. Slowly one person here opened his eyes and another there; one person here stopped tapping and clapping and another there. Finally Mugia and Maria opened their eyes and slowly stopped dancing. For a moment there was an embarrassed silence, the kind of silence that a child shows when he is discovered relieving himself in the wrong place. Mugia roared into a hearty laughter of relief, victory and joy. Everybody joined him in a mixed chorus, the man patting him on the shoulder and the women looking at him with eyes burning with desire. Even Ntanya was laughing. There was no mistaking it, these were happy people.

Only two people did not share in this agitation. The old man was still sleeping by the wall; in his open mouth a fly was doing its own dance. It is hard to imagine how one could sleep at this moment, but then he was an old, bald man, and Teresa was no longer sitting on his lap. Teresa too seemed to be apart from all this. Still leaning on Ntanya she was staring at the setting sun. Her eyes seemed to be absorbed by it, and once in a while a wave of convulsions would go through her from below, silently and powerfully, culminating in her bosom and shoulders. The laughing crowd was unaware of her; she was unaware of them. It is difficult to know what worried her. She was probably just afraid of the setting sun, as many people are. Maybe she was afraid that it might not come up again, and even if it did, the interim of darkness might frighten her − all those things that happen in darkness, things of darkness, the consequences of which we have to face in the sun. Who knows? She could be in terror or merely in a violent anticipation. The heart of a human being is a dark universe. She could even have discovered an underlying truth about herself, about her future and, like everybody else, have been frightened by it.

The laughing had stopped and the ensuing silence tapered slowly into a regrouping of small drinking committees talking quietly and wiping sweat from their faces with dirty fingers. Darkness was quickly setting in and the middle-aged woman, the one to be Ntanya's and who had disappeared all this time, came in in a great hurry looking rather flustered though with a calm face. She started struggling to light the three lanterns that were hanging on a wooden hook on the mud wall, meanwhile mumbling something or other to herself.

A bright light flashed across the room and disappeared, and flashed again getting brighter and brighter. A car pulled up by the entrance. Maria who had disappeared into the partition with Mugia rushed back to the sitting room. It would be the police. 'Bastards, lousy bastards,' she said out aloud. The only people she really hated were the police. They never said what should not be done. They were not intelligent enough for that. They were full of what should not be done at a particular place, in a particular way. Everybody scrambled to hide himself; even the old man, who had been stepped on and who had the headlights glaring in his eyes, got up, thinking himself in hell or heaven and knelt down to pray till he got back his senses. He then got up, ran in confusion hither and thither like a laying chicken and finally ducked behind the door – a stupid place to hide. Maria stood there unperturbed with her arms akimbo, waiting. Mugia stood behind her with a club dangling from his hand. Teresa was leaning on Ntanya, her eyes still fixed at the point where the sun had disappeared into its nocturnal sleep.

Two men in dark glasses came out of the car. Mugia roared into a laugh, unable to finish his sentence, 'They are just Government Officers, not the police.' The hiders came out relieved, and the old man walking gingerly to his seat said quietly in relief, 'I always said that there are only two points where the whole of mankind meets, sex and death.' Laughter greeted the newcomers.

Coming in, they felt embarrassed especially as Teresa, still absorbed in thought or meditation, did not move an inch and they had to squeeze themselves in through the little available space. Everybody was staring at them with suspicion and hatred. It was abundantly clear that they were not welcome; after all this was not a government office and they too should be required to say 'Sir' and stand in a queue.

Looking around the room, one of them set his eyes on Ntanya, took off his glasses and – my God! – it was James. Finding a straw to hang on, he affected surprise, yelling, 'Why we've been looking for you all evening.' Ntanya saw through the lie and smiled, half-contemptuously extending his arm to give his 'friend' a bridge to these people who no longer felt at ease, the very people James despised by day but searched for and dreamt about at night.

The customers were no longer happy and had stopped talking; they were probably afraid of what the Government Officers might say about unemployment or village development or maybe even about death. So Mugia fumbled in his pocket and, fetching out his last coin, ordered a calabash for each. They bowed to him gratefully with understanding and started drinking quickly without resting the calabashes or sharing them, as if they had not touched a drop that day. Even the newcomers got a calabash. They took white handkerchiefs out of their pockets and covered the stone at the corner and sat down. Teresa, who was no longer in contemplation, and had been staring at the scar beneath James's eye, laughed out aloud. All the eyes were turned to her. She checked herself without much feeling and shrugged her shoulders.

James ordered another calabash for everybody and yet others, though nobody seemed grateful and nobody seemed to bow with understanding the way they had done with Mugia's offer. They drank it all the same, partly because it is bad manners to turn down a gift and partly because the previous ones were not without effect even on Ntanya and James himself. As the effect increased the bridge between the two groups narrowed. They were now talking loudly about this and that. The old man was loudest of all, recounting broken bits of his history or his imagined history, though nobody seemed to be listening, not even Teresa who was now sitting on Mugia's lap. The millet brew seemed to release particularly profound eloquence from James. As soon as the old man, running from the mouth in

43

excitement and eloquence, stopped, James would start. One moment he would play Hamlet without an audience. The next he was quoting the Gospel or fragments of the Bible. Suddenly, he started listening keenly to the old man's pathetic story, ending in tears, telling how he had moved north, reconfirming what had only been a rumour. He wet Maria's hand in gratitude. Teresa went over to him and kneeling by him tried to stop him from talking. She knew how much the wound he was scratching hurt and would hurt, and she also knew that this portended no good for the old man. He had never told anybody the story of his rise and fall and now that he was telling it to the public he would fall completely, for one cannot skin himself and live. He refused to stop. 'My darling daughter, my angel,' he said caressing her hair. 'It is my day of reckoning. I have to pay up. Don't stop me. I'll say everything – everything. You can be a mistress for me, you can say that he at least understood where the chain broke, understood why he had to die in a brothel.' Everybody started with amazement and guilt. 'Yes, you can say he spoke the truth at last. That he died a wise man. For what is wisdom but to find out on the death bed where the chain broke, to find out retrogressively how things could have been? Impotent as it is, it is great consolation.' Everybody was now standing around him as people do after an accident.

Teresa, weeping herself, was drying the old man's tears with the corner of her gown. 'Please father don't, don't,' she pleaded.

He continued to turn himself round and round on the dissection table of his mind. He missed no detail, not even the colour of the dress worn by the girl he had jilted the last time he had seen her. He told how he had decided to live the life of a sex troubadour knowing full well, right from the beginning, how he would end. This last point he emphasised as if in victory over a completed job. After pausing a little in exhaustion he went on, 'Does it really make a difference how one lived, so long as one is living? At the end one has to look back, to settle accounts. I have settled my accounts in tears and I've nothing to regret.' He fell into a paroxysm of sobbing. Sighs of grief were heard all around the room. Everybody was as moved as if the old man had been talking about their own lives. The effect of the beer had evaporated. They stood there gazing at the ground or at the old man, or closing their eyes and looking inwards. Only the two Government Officers looked different. James was talking about something or other. In the most unnatural fashion a fragment of information rolled over in his mind and of course he had to let it out to a stupefied audience, drowning the old man's sobs and lacerations, 'The world is a round stool where old men sit and twist their grey moustaches until they get sores on their bottoms and turn around to listen to the story of how each other's lives could have been. How tiring it is to sit on a stool and twist one's moustache when one is bald and ...' Everybody was looking at him with a mouth wide in amazement, feeling he had either gone mad or he was insulting them. Mugia lost his temper, and rushed forward. He grabbed James by the shoulder and threw him out of the door like an impudent dog. His fellow Government Officer followed him. They started the car without putting on the headlights and left.

Ntanya felt guilty about having been associated with James today, especially since all the eyes were accusingly thrown at him. In the meantime the old man had fallen into a sort of a coma, and it was obvious that he did not have long to go. Maria and Teresa were trying to pick him up to put him to bed. Everybody should die in bed. Seeing them struggle Ntanya rushed over to help, partly because everybody else was too surprised to even know that their help was needed, and partly because Ntanya wanted to alleviate the guilt of having been known by James.

When Ntanya, Teresa and Maria came back to the sitting room, people started going out one by one, slowly and quietly as if the ground hurt. They all disappeared into the darkness. Unlike the young man, who that day had walked out tying his loin-cloth and laughing, they all walked back downcast. Maybe they were even sadder than when they had come in. Their greedy desires were unsatisfied, maybe even atrophied by the fear that been laying ambush to their hearts all the time and whose raw sting was now exposed bare, though unintentionally, by the old man's self-lacerations. Even the Government Officers walked out with their desires tied around their loins, and their airy authority mortified for, after all, they had been kicked out like dogs. Unlike the others, however, they had not had the dream world of their knowledge shattered, and sorrow and fear were not resting on their shoulders. It was just another peasant who was going to die; and as James had once commented cynically in public, 'This country will never be cleared up and will never progress until all these tribal superstition-ridden peasants have died.' Maybe it was just a quotation, for James was a learned man. But whatever it was, many peasants remembered him on their death beds.

The last person to leave was Ntanya. Completely bewildered, he did not even hear Maria say goodnight. Teresa, just as flustered, followed him behind into the darkness after standing confused at the door, looking at Maria and then at the darkness outside, pleading for understanding from both. Teresa followed Ntanya. He was completely unaware of his follower, and moved on in a straight line unaware of where he was going. 'I just wanted to tell ...' Ntanya started out of a dream and looked back, but there was only darkness around him. 'I wanted to tell you that I can't come with you tonight though I would love to. That old man is dying and he needs me at his bedside. I want to see you again, soon.' As soon as she finished she rushed back, and a moment later Ntanya saw a black dot disappearing into the yellow light of the house. Ntanya stood there for some time without comprehending the full significance of those words, repeating aloud over and over to himself, 'I want to sec you again, soon.'

When Ntanya got home he found the whole family around his dying father, much in the way that everybody had congregated around the old man at Maria's house. His father was writhing in pain and breathing with difficulty as if the whole world was resting on his dehydrated consumptive chest. Once in a while he would raise his arms in desperation and kick as if to drive off this weight, this demon, and then he would go into a fit of rending coughing. When Ntanya entered the small door of his father's hut, the family turned to him, not in accusation but with expectation, as if they thought he would save the dying man. His unseeing mother somehow felt his presence without asking. Ntanya touched her on the shoulder and she understood. She relinquished her place and Ntanya sat at the top of the bedstead and supported his father's troubled head on his lap. He noticed in the dark light of the kerosene burner that they had all been crying.

The mother whispered to the children, 'Let's go to sleep now, children, let's go to sleep, Ntanya is here.' All the children, exhausted by the emptiness of their tears followed her obediently as chicks follow a hen. The youngest brother held her hand. Onya threw an affectionate look at her brother, patted him on the shoulder, and she too walked out. She came back a few moments later with a bowl of meat, a gourd full of curdled milk and the boiled sweet potatoes that Ntanya liked so much. Ntanya had no appetite at a moment like this, but Onya cut the meat into small pieces, stuck them in his mouth with pieces of potatoes, and even held the gourd to his mouth. She would have chewed for him if that was possible, so great was her love for her brother. Ntanya chewed and swallowed mechanically and, unaware, let the rich cold milk wash down the potatoes and meat. After Ntanya had shaken his head to signal his satisfaction, Onya collected the half-full vessels together and made as if to go out. Suddenly she threw a look at her father who was asleep, and a longer one at her brother. She rested her arm on her brother's shoulders, and with a profound noise between a sigh and a sob softly and gracefully walked out without even saying goodnight.

Everybody has got his night, the night when everything comes to a sharp point like a boil. After that night life reaches a climax, and the rest is just a summing-up, a going downhill through a road, well-known because it has been travelled before. It is true some people are lucky enough to be able to manage to sleep through this night. But some born with their eyes open keep vigil through the night to watch every move, every twitch of pain, lest they forget to retrace their way downhill and get called upon for another night like this.

Ntanya was no exception. Now was the night of the lone naked soul. After tonight all would be a summing-up, though an unpredictable summing-up, for metal can be so over-heated that it may lose its elasticity and become brittle. The little kerosene container would soon dry up. The flame was already stumbling this way and that way in weakness and thirst on the red ember that was originally torn out of the rags of Ntanya's young brother's old herding dress. The flame would soon die. There it went. The air is quite still. Even the owls have deserted Ntanya. There is only darkness and the laboured breathing of the dying man, his father.

After the light went off Ntanya kept staring at the embers, until that little flicker was swallowed up in the great darkness. Even after this his eyes were still fixed at the point which had become merely a stretch of darkness where a light burnt some time before. It was strange that he could open his eyes in this total darkness when it did not make any difference whether or not his eyes were open. Probably the strongest thing was his mind. Up to now he had been running around with his mind foggy. Was it really light or darkness that itched inside him to be let out? He had been running around dazed in an illusion, a luxury of not understanding, like a child sullen because he had been scolded and not beaten. Now his mind surprised him with its clarity and defeated acceptance. He sat there aware of everything, in a state beyond fear, with his father's head still resting on his lap.

In this distilled awareness he closed his eyes and clenched his fists not so much in irritation, though he was sweating in the cool of the night, but in concentration. With his father's head in his lap, still warm with life but quivering in the weakness of last moments, Ntanya's mind started soaring high above the ground of his past life. Like an eagle flying over a burnt grassland, he had many spots to look at, many places on which to come down. Years or even seconds of a human experience are so complex that one can never choose what to re-examine, any more than one originally chose the experience. When people talk about choosing an experience in the past or future they either mean that the particular experience chose them or else that they picked the experience blind-folded and at random, as when one sticks a hand into a pot in the dark and pulls out a cockroach. For an experience has too many shadows or probabilities, the complexities of which were probably not meant to be deciphered by the human mind or heart. Ntanya was an exception. He was looking for something, a lost seed on a wilderness of burnt grass. What was going to direct him? Where was he going to land?

He could alight on the day when as a little boy, so many experiences ago, he had been counting the number of Mapani bees that settled on a Nandi flame flower on a hot afternoon; suddenly and without reason it had started to rain. Was there anything there? He could have alighted on the day when, after bitterness had infected his time in the town, he had gone to bed with an ageing prostitute and, instead of paying her, had beaten her and burnt her clothes. Could there be something there? Possibly not; a person suffering from tuberculosis cannot find its cause.

His mind roamed on and on till out of sheer tiredness (with his eyes shut he was sweating profusely) it alighted on ground so bleak that his mind had dubiously looked around it (all the time he was involuntarily caressing his father's calm head).

It was many years ago. He did not know how many, for he did not remember numbers, only events. Unlike years which necessarily follow each other, events sometimes come isolated in spurts.

One day a few years after his mother had died, Ntanya had woken up not feeling well. His neck was sore, his guts were constipated and his mind blurred foggy by a dream about his mother. He had dreamt of his mother rushing to him as he lay bleeding after a fall. He felt suspended like a word at the beginning of an unknown sentence. The desire for life or death hung in the sun to dry. It was one of those days when one drifts aimlessly from this to that because bitterness, despair, love or hatred has set one free from the constant compulsion of passion. Ntanya drifted that day through a morning. The details were no longer too clear since many layers of burnt grass covered the disconnected events of the day. It had been a wet and muddy morning. He had the usual two mile walk to the school which he was to attend for four years. There was more rain and thunder. Being free from himself, he had neither had his breakfast, nor bothered to cut a banana leaf to protect himself from the rain. The question was why had he drifted to school at all? Why the school? Why not the market or to the forest? Or to the stupid-looking mud hut that the foreigners, the worshippers of disintegration of the body, had built just so that they could pray for the rain all day when it was raining through the holed roof? Does a school have a special magnet for people who are drifting, people who have been lost in the desert?

It was just as wet in the school house as it was outside. The difference was that the rain was brown with the colour of rotting grass thatch. As a punishment for being late, Ntanya had to stand in the corner where it rained most, after four strokes which he did not feel or mind. The teacher was quite an interesting young man. He was charming in his own way and amusing in the purity of his ignorance.

Even at moments like this Ntanya's mind could remember some other fragments of that day's happening. The teacher was short and of a groundnut colour; his stomach protruded less and less as the day went on. He was renowned for his zeal and academic enthusiasm. He once boasted of being a member of that cardless universal association of producers and consumers of knowledge, though he volunteered to say gladly that he was more on the consumer side. He taught with vigour and violence, partly to hide the fact that he could not do anything else, and partly because he really did believe that he was making better men of these boys. He taught everything in the four-year course that was supposed to change savages into civilised men, though he himself only licked tongues at civilisation. He was in an arithmetic lesson talking about cube roots. Ntanya could have sat down if he had known precisely how to answer the question thrown at him: 'What's the cube root of the square root of one over nine?' He could have just as well asked Ntanya the colour of God or the day he would die. He would have been more able to reply. Ntanya had simply looked at the teacher, shivering not from fear but from cold, and had quietly said he did not know. He had wanted to add aloud that he did not care about cube roots. But just then he had noticed that his wet calico had stuck on his front parts and he struggled to free himself from the calico. This disregard set the teacher raving and Ntanya's backside received another warming. To his surprise Ntanya did not react at all.

He stood there just as before looking at the brown rain from which the teacher was protected by a corrugated iron sheet. Ntanya wished so much that he could tell his dream to the teacher and to the class. He wished that there was a school where he could talk about his dreams, about the sensation he was now feeling of the brown rain dripping down on his clothes making them stick to his body. What did he have to do with cube roots after he had dreamt that his mother came to rescue him in his accident?

Class had ended, and walking by him the teacher shook his head in despair. He had realised that Ntanya was one of those boys who did not belong in school. He was one of those who always asked why and who ended up by committing suicide, running mad or becoming great. But he was only a teacher and his knowledge ended with a cube root. Here it had failed him. The teacher turned to Ntanya again and said that if he did not fall back into step he was afraid he was going to send him home. Ntanya was about to say that he was not even going to come back to this place again, but something stopped him. Maybe it was just because he was too busy looking at the clean rain falling outside.

Ntanya had walked straight from the school to his mother's grave. It was still fresh and wet and not a seed had grown. He sat down on the mud with his hands resting on the raised mound and cried. His tears mixed with the rain and dripped on to the mound until there were no tears left. After it had stopped raining he had drifted homewards. He knew that he could never go back to that school again. He could never learn roots now after crying at his mother's grave. It was as if sitting on the grave had washed him clean of boyhood, clean of being a lover of knowledge about division and multiplication, the Chinese Revolution, or the Massif Central. The tears he shed there had even washed him clean of ordinary sensations, hopes and cares. What did anything really matter if his mother was living deep in the ground with her mouth full of mud? His mother had once said that it was not death of which she was afraid; that was only a sensual point in time; she was afraid of the absence after death, the lull that follows an extinguished fire. Now that fire that had generated so much warmth was extinguished, did anything else burn? Could one be expected to work in darkness? Ntanya at that time had both hated and despised those people who work in darkness, and who wear imaginary cloth which is dissolved by light. It was like learning arithmetic that is necessarily found useless unless one could find the cube root of the unsatisfied whims and desires that lay embalmed underneath or frozen at a grave. One could of course play games in the dark. But a game that is mistaken for work is bad work. This is of course what most people were doing in the world, especially those in school and the success lot. They were avoiding the real issue, studying and following the bad shadows of real objects; for objects in real life have good and bad shadows and most of them are bad. All those serious boys in there must have had something to say that was really important to them the way their mothers had looked at them last night, with their fear of losing her one day or losing themselves. The teacher could tell the class how his stomach receded and receded with time, only to be paunchy again on the following day. That must have made a difference for him. No, that is irrelevant. It is not on the syllabus. God forbid that it will ever become relevant to you or to the syllabus makers. But it will one day; quickly like lightning you will be caught unawares standing with your head between your legs to observe the illusion of the moon; the rug will be pulled from underneath; then like all of them you will start to rave, kick and play, and there will be only your work-play of darkness, which will evaporate in the light.

He had been saying a prayer in his mind as he walked along, not to anybody or any god in particular. The deepest of our prayers are never really said to God or anybody in particular; they simply come as incoherently broken desires and hopes that can never be verbalised.

He tried to remember it. He could not remember the details. Important events have a tendency of losing the trivial trappings and leaving only the bold fundamentals. A man often remembers only the eternal sound in the throat of the woman he last made love to, not the colour of her dress. Ntanya remembered wishing, with all he had, that he should not follow bad shadows, that he should not mistake a game for work, and that he should not get caught unaware. He had said before that with death nothing made any difference. But now he knew something did make a difference — awareness. A soldier does not really defeat another if his foe, dying under the weight of a spear, dies looking at him when he has speared him from behind when fleeing. Something did make a difference. Something gave a core to his work-play. For this awareness he had been ready to swap anything else, any amount of difficulties and pain.

Could it have been here? Could his prayers have been answered by the unknown that he had addressed them to? Is this what awareness meant — an awareness that is stripped of even the knowledge of itself? He was then only a boy and he had not seen Mugia dance. Was he bound by his silent prayer, if a pre-condition of it had been an understanding of this awareness he still longed for? Could the child asking for fish have much later had a snake pushed into his mouth?.

His search in the unfamiliar and terrible map of his history was abruptly ended by a violent movement of the head on his lap and, coming back to his father's hut, he realised that two or three owls had been singing to the north of the hut. He also noticed that a breeze had risen and that the leaves of the bananas that thatched the hut were rustling. He fumbled in the dark looking for the gourd of water. Dying people are always given water when they make any movement, much as a crying baby has a nipple automatically thrust in his mouth. Maybe the dying man did not want any water, maybe he just wanted to move his head without reason, to prove that he could do so as a last gesture of revolt against God and death. Dying people

54

should always behave with reason. At least they should ask for water, for Thales was not that stupid after all. Ntanya remembered one day a woman torn by despair after the death of her only son saying, 'Why, my little son did not even drink the water I held to his lips. Not even the water held by his poor widowed mother. Why do these things happen, God? Why I ask you? But I guess you don't know either.' And she had slumped back into her despair. Maybe she was right. God did not know either. After all they say that his own son had died while he just looked on, and that he had not even offered him water. He had looked on, maybe, too moved with grief, and allowed enemies to give his son bitter water.

Ntanya found the gourd and on his way back he hit his head badly against the middle post. He then felt for the old man's lips. How dry they were and how lifeless. The old man drank quickly like a dry cow-hide soaking. Yes, he drank the water out of his son's hands and went back to sleep. For the water was not bitter. Ntanya resumed his former position after having himself drunk out of the same gourd putting his lips at the same point that his father had, not because he was thirsty, but because, well he did not know why. Maybe his father too had drunk without thirst. Just because the water was offered him by his son and maybe he drank because of Thales. To the health of Thales, ladies and gentlemen! Did Thales too drink water before he died? Probably not. That would have been blasphemous, and he was a very wet holy man.

With his father's head calm on his lap, his mind started wandering again. But he could no longer think straight. The owls were too loud in their festival. His head was aching. The breeze had changed into a monsoon. He fell asleep with his head leaning on the wall and his father's head in his lap.

So passed Ntanya's night of darkness. Did he have many such nights left? Or was his whole life after that day in the rain at his mother's grave one long such night? His mother (or should we start calling her what she really was, his grandmother?) came in led by Onya, carrying two bowls of banana soup for her sick children. The men were still asleep. She touched Ntanya on the forehead just where he had hit himself the night before. For she could not see anything at all and she could only feel. Ntanya jumped in pain, practically knocking the dying man off the bed. He stood a step or two from the bed, not really knowing where he was or what had happened. The two women struggled to roll back the dying man, and to prevent him from falling down. Ntanya only stood there gazing at them, mopping with his fingers the blood from the freshened wound that had not hurt the night before. Ntanya looked at the blood on his hands as if he had never seen blood before; or maybe he was just concentrating on his vague outline reflected in it. The two women were busy, the grandmother fed the sick man slowly with a wooden spoon and the sister tidied up the bed, while explaining to her sighing grandmother what had happened. Ntanya got a piece of a broken mirror from under the bed, wiped it and looked at himself. He had not looked at himself in a mirror for a long time. It was as if he was looking at his image that had been sketched by somebody else years later. He looked so old and tired. He checked his head nervously. It is said that one can grow grey-haired overnight. But he had not.

The old man was lying out in the sun propped up by a banana leaf pillow that Onya had quickly fashioned and covered with an old blanket. He looked much better that morning. Though he still could not talk or eat his condition was far from hopeless. His mother was quite excited with new hopes of her son coming back to life and, though normally a woman of few words, she chattered on to Onya who sat in the shade of the banana tree scouring with ashes a tin pot that would not get white since she was absent-mindedly scrubbing at only one point, and on the outside at that.

'I told you, daughter, one should never lose heart. Never lose hope in God. He is going to walk right out of here, just like the strong baby he was. And he was a strong baby, you little devil you.' She caressed her son's face, very carefully as if suddenly he had become only a week old. With the infinite tenderness of which the remains of her maternal love was capable, she pushed the cloth that covered him down to the waist, not to look at the bony chest since she had no sight left, but to allow the sun to do so. 'Yes daughter, he was so strong. One day he practically pulled off my breast while suckling just because he had lost his temper.' She started laughing her toothless laugh and shaking in her weariness and hope. 'But you know it was good those days. It hurt much, but what is pain when one was so happy and full.' She touched her empty breasts and shook her head. 'No, pain was nothing those days. Why his father was just as much of a child as him; desire and violence, violence and desire. He would have suckled too if I'd allowed him to. Men are all children, you know.'

Onya who had stopped scrubbing the pot and was looking at her brother had not really been listening to her, but she simply replied, 'Yes mother, they are.'

'We must feed our children today. We must feed them well. Why I thought your father was going to die, but God has brought him back. I swear before we finish cooking he will be walking, and you know people who come that close to death wake up very hungry. Go my daughter, go to the Mirisho's house and ask Gagawa to lend us a chicken. Tell her we'll bring another one back tomorrow — you can go and sell the millet tomorrow and then we'll buy another one. We must feed our children well today, so that they won't say their women folk let them down.'

'Oh, but mother, Gagawa died two years ago and you know it,' replied Onya who had trembled a bit when her grandmother talked of Gagawa.

'Oh my God, yes. Why they even sent me the burial meat. What is happening to me my daughter? Am I really getting that old?'

'No mother, we all forget at times.' Silence crept in. It always does when one mentions somebody one once knew who is now dead. The mother turned around as if in shame to face the son she could not see, and put her hand on the son's face. Onya was still gazing at Ntanya who sat facing west with his head between his thighs. He was playing with the soil, letting it drip slowly through his finger like a sand-clock, then starting all over again and again with deliberation and regularity. Whenever he did that Onya knew that he was either in meditation or just lost. This time he was not there at all. Neither was he meditating about anything in particular. He was just lost. His consciousness and care had left him suspended in mid-air sifting sand between his thighs. He had not even heard his grandmother when she talked. Even now he did not hear his sister asking him with the tenderness and love that she was so capable of, what he was doing. There are times when we look without seeing, turn our ears without hearing. Though Onya's question was left in the air she knew that it did not mean she was being rejected. She first went over to Ntanya, patted him on the shoulder and then to tell the children either not to make so much noise or else to go further away to play. Then she busied herself cleaning and preparing the noon meal. The meal today must be good. She went over to a pot at the corner of the hut and dug out the three shillings which she had saved for two years in the hope that one day she would save enough to be able to buy herself a beautiful dress. She knew she was a pretty girl and, being a hard worker as well, she was sure when the time came she would find it easy to get a good husband; but since men are dreamers she would also have to wear a beautiful dress to fortify her beauty, and at sixteen this was just the time. That had been two years before. She had then hoped that Ntanya would settle down and take care of the young ones, or that her father would remarry. Now that Ntanya had not settled down, and that her father was at the point of death, what difference could a new dress make? She called her brother and sent him to Mirisho's house to buy a chicken, though not without feeling that somebody had pulled something out of her heart.

'Oh, I wish there was meat today,' the old soul sitting in the shade with the men, was saying as Onya handed her the bowl with the biggest part of the chicken. She always got the first serving and the biggest share not only because she had the biggest bag of a stomach and a boy's appetite, but because she was the eldest. Onya always told the protesting young ones, 'She's old. She will die before you, so you have a lot more food to go. Besides, without her, where would we be?'

'There's meat, mother, chicken,' Onya replied as she directed the old woman's hand to the spoon. 'But you said Gagawa is dead,' she said with a mouth full. The pulped maize and chicken gravy lay underneath the meat, which, she being toothless, swallowed whole. She was so busy with her food that she did not hear Onya say that there were other Gagawas.

Onya went to feed the father, carefully, sticking the spoon full of gravy and little pieces of chicken in his mouth, while her younger brother held the bowl. The old man had indeed recovered. He shook his head when satisfied and Onya washed the chicken down his throat with milk held to his mouth, but which dripped on to the old man's neck. When she then took Ntanya's bowl to him he shook his head, even after Onya had knelt down begging him to eat. Grandmother, who had been busy with her bowl, also joined in. 'Eat, my son, it is good food and your father is going to live now. Eat from the gentle hands of your sister. She's the best cook in Kachawanga. A full stomach always chases away sorrow. Eat.' And she ducked her head back to her bowl, unaware of Ntanya's final shaking of his head.

Onya moved with the remains of her three shillings in the pot over to the other side of the tree. She picked up the wing of a chicken but, before it touched her lips, she put it back and started crying quietly. Ntanya noticed this, walked over to her, put his hand on her shoulder and started eating roughly and mechanically, chewing chicken bone, maize and gravy all in one as though a bitter medicinal herb. Onya dried her tears and started eating slowly, but she was hurt, deeply hurt. She did not blame her brother but she had given all she had and it had not been appreciated. Can one, even by a brother, be asked to do more than one is capable of?

As the sun moved more and more to the west, and the shadows of the banana trees weighed the hut down, the hopes of the mother faded. Except for Ntanya they had moved back to the sunshine on a little patch between the shadows. Onya was whispering to the mother periodic reports of how the sick man was doing. They were not good. The glaze of life that had once again brightened his face that morning was receding. He periodically shivered as his lips moved, unable to say anything, not even 'My.' If only he could have said, 'My,' his mother would have jumped with thanksgiving. But he did not say anything. He just feebly moved his lips. He could not have been asking for water either, since Ntanya's youngest brother had been kneeling there with a full gourd tipping it to the moving lips at a signal from Onya. So the mother sat there rigidly with her brows knit, witnessing her excitement and hope die slowly, like a person withdrawing a smile that has mistakenly been given to a despising enemy.

Ntanya was seated as before, letting sand drift through his

fingers over and over again. Once in a while he licked his lips as if nothing was happening around him. Once in a while his buttocks would hurt and then he would recline on his elbow for a time before going back to his former position. Once in a while he would throw a glance at the rest of the family; but it would be like somebody looking at a cob of maize on the ground.

The youngest sister came rushing in. She too was no party to what was going on. She was only eager to deliver the message she carried. 'Somebody's waiting for you at the pathway, big brother. It's a woman, a young girl, and she says it's urgent. She's crying.' She repeated this twice, but seeing that Ntanya did not notice she ran over and patted him on the head repeating the message. Ntanya started, saying 'Eh?' The child repeated the message again quickly with irritation and ended by saying as she ran back to her play that Ntanya should use his ears.

Ntanya dragged himself up slowly and walked towards the entrance. He went a few steps and came back, took the gourd and tried to give his father water but he would not drink. He put the gourd back in the hands of his brother and walked out to the entrance without looking back. Teresa was standing crying at the entrance hidden behind the white-ant mound. She fell on his chest crying more violently without saying anything.

Ntanya put his arms around Teresa silently. When she was too weak to stand he picked her up and sat down with her sitting on his lap, still crying. At last when she had finished, she held Ntanya's face in her hands and looked at him closely, and started saying 'He's dead. He died this afternoon. Oh it was so horrible. We stayed up all night with him. And then this morning he lost his mind and started raving about this and that. Why he even said I killed him by sitting on your lap yesterday. He even said. . .' She started crying again, but quickly straightened herself up and looked Ntanya in the eyes pleadingly. 'Do you really think I killed him?'

Ntanya, who had been sitting there holding her much the same way he had let dust trickle through his fingers a little while before, said 'No, Teresa, you did not kill him. Nobody kills anybody. People die either because they want to or because they have to.'

Teresa was not reassured. 'Maybe if I had remained on his lap he would not have wanted to die.'

Ntanya was letting dust trickle through his fingers on his left hand again and simply replied 'Maybe!'

They sat there for some time. Suddenly Teresa stood up as if she had completely recovered, and gazed down on Ntanya. 'This is the hot season and the flies are many, we must bury him this evening. If we wait till tomorrow he may have started . . . to smell. Come and help us. Maria and Mugia are quite beside themselves. Please come and help us.'

It was no easy job for the two men as it was still hot. Yet they did not however feel like asking for help. At least Maria did not. There was something of a family affair in this undertaking like interring a still-born child or diseased donkey. They worked efficiently and quietly, without ceremony, without even a soothsayer. The women were seated in the shade of the tree watching the men heave and sweat. Soon the nameless old man was sinking slowly, and yet so far down he would never have to sink further. When he had lain in the shade covered in his old blanket, the only thing which he had left, his death had not yet attained a rigid finality. But as he started going down in the hole in the ground the women started sobbing again, Teresa punctuating her weeping with 'Ho! ho!' as if somebody was hitting her in the stomach.

The men finished their job without exchanging a word. They dusted their hands and their jembes on the grass. But they had forgotten to mark the grave. Every grave must be marked so that when people walk by they may hang their head in solemn remembrance of the dead or of their own death. The men were too tired to remember to put a mark on this grave, but women never forget such things. Maria rolled a stone, too big for her with her weeping breasts, slowly and painfully to the head of the grave. Teresa was not there to help her. She had run to fetch the dead man's bronze mask from the wall in the house. He must have used it in masquerading during his younger days. It had struck her during her tears that it would be nice to stick the old man's mask on his grave. Do they not stick the spear and shield of a soldier killed in action on his grave? So the two women cut a branch of a tree, stuck it into the ground next to Maria's stone, and hung on it the bronze mask. Then they followed their men into the house. People who passed by, for it was not too far from the dirt road, laughed out aloud, thinking this to be a joke by Muteta the village clown or somebody.

When the passers-by got home they spread the story of the fresh soil with a mask on it and the whole village shook with laughter; even Ntanya's mother who had been sad all day laughed until she cried. A few weeks later rumours spread in the village that the nameless old man had in fact buried his old blanket, left his mask there, and moved on to another village to the north, that one day he would tip over the end of the earth-table. This was many years ago, and like any other village Kachawanga tends to forget funny stories. Just the other day, however, I was passing by the old man's grave. A small Catholic church is going up near there. A large tree has grown out of Maria's twig and the bronze mask is squashed out of all pro-portion by the tree branches. One can however still see its smile crushed into a sneer by the growing tree. As I stopped to look, an amicable Catholic father, the type who plays Christ all his life, with that golden beard for hiding the boy behind it, joined me to look at the mask and, after saying 'Praised be the Virgin,' and crossing himself, started addressing me in that holy-water sweetness. 'There is so much to be discovered in Africa. This tree springs from deep down so many African civilizations, a symbol, a witness to the fact I have always believed that you were superior to us long ago and that the pride of your superiority made God smite as he smote the Gomorrans. Yes, this archaeological mushroom is a miracle, a most holy miracle, praise be to the virgin, and that is why we are building this church here as a humble acknowledgement of entreaty.' I said 'Yes, father,' and moved on. I ignored his request to stay for the evening mass under the tree as I was angry because the picture I was trying to conjure up of this tragic old man had been broken once and for all. Stop there some time before the Catholic church is finished, for they might cut down the tree and put the mask as a holy relic on the altar.

When the women got back to the hut they found the men seated, looking down, with sweat still dripping from their tired bodies. Maria brought a bowl of beer for each, for after a death one's throat gets dry. Mugia swallowed his in a gulp and looked down again. Ntanya and Teresa only shook their heads, and then Maria handed Ntanya's to Mugia and had two for herself.

Ntanya started homewards without saying a word. Teresa, who had been following his steps like a hungry dog following the movement of a piece of meat being dangled, tore herself from her stool and ran after Ntanya. She reached him at the very spot where she had caught up with him the night before. 'Take me with you. Please Ntanya take me with you. I can't live with Maria any more. I can't live in that house of death. I haven't anywhere else to go. Please take me with you. I'm not asking you to make me your wife or one of them; although if you did you would have no dowry to pay or anything. I'll wash your feet every morning and night. And I can cook; I can cook a very good banana stew. My mother taught me how before she

64

died. I'll keep your bed warm and give you a back-rub when you are tired. I saw your beautiful little sister today. Maybe you have more brothers and sisters. I'll take care of them, wash them and mend their calico. I'm good at that too. I'll even find herbs for their stomach worms; my father taught me that before he died. I'll even raise your big fat babies – I will I will if you allow me to. Oh how I should love to carry your babies in me and then on my back. Please take me with you Ntanya, please!'

This entreaty, spoken in extreme nervousness with words quickly running into each other like a hurriedly rehearsed speech fell like raindrops on the back of a duck. Since last night Ntanya had not been hearing much: He was not there. He did not know where he was. Teresa took this to be a rebuff. But in desperation she was not easily put off, so she pushed in front of Ntanya and knelt before him, clinging to his legs. Looking at him there up above her, with those beautiful brown goat-eyes of hers swollen in tears, she said slowly and with tear-mellowed deliberation, pronouncing each word carefully, 'Taa fadhali unichukuwe, tafadhali. Please take me with you, please.' There was no bitterness or rejection in Ntanya's eyes. There are certain images that although we see only once, we can never shake out of our memories, never until we die. The power of the image of Ntanya today, towering up above her in that celestial illusion. It was one that Teresa was never to forget until a twig marked her bed.

Ntanya who was looking down at her had heard only the last 'Please take me with you.' He helped her up and put his arm around her waist. It was not a bad waist he put his arm on. They started moving homewards away from the setting sun.

At times, even possibly most of the time, the flesh is much wiser than the spirit, just as children are at times so much wiser than adults. When Ntanya put his arm around this girl, it was as if he was rubbing off a dream from his natural eyes. It had been the rhythm of Mugia's dancing the night before that had started this awakening. A simmering had remained there growing, growing slowly in the darkness of that dreadful night, but in his anguish he had not noticed it. As he had sat there in the sun sifting sand, this hope, hope deep in the flesh, had been growing all the time; slowly and steadily it had been drawing heat from the ashes of his frustrated soul like babies born to lame mothers after the defeat of war. As he put his arm around Teresa it proclaimed itself loudly in desire that was more than sensual. More, because he had put his arms around women's waists before; indeed he had done with them many times those dreadful things which always made the back of his mouth taste sour on the following day. He was now on the threshold of a completely new type of experience. Putting his arm around Teresa's waist was like sitting at his mother's grave beneath the holly tree. He just wanted to leave it there and go on moving east, much as he had felt like sitting at his mother's grave, just sitting there unaware of anything else but his mother talking to him in those silent discussions of present memory.

He was walking very fast, unaware of Teresa's short steps; she had to half-run to keep up with him and make him hear what she had to say, 'I've gone to bed with only three men at Maria's. I had to, believe me, Ntanya, I had to. One was a government official, one of those with big cars. I didn't want to but Maria needed the money and I needed Maria to survive. The other one forced me. Oh, it was so horrible I wanted to kill myself if I was ever to carry his baby but fortunately I didn't. The other one was the man who died. He threatened to kill himself if I didn't allow him to play with me. I didn't mind that very much; I hear that in some places they donate blood to save people who're dying. Do you think it was wrong for me to, Ntanya?'

Ntanya was still walking fast. It was as if, being too suddenly filled with Teresa, he was unaware of her, and was just laughing out aloud. God knows when he last laughed that boisterously, and with a note of so much happiness. In fact when

Teresa, tugging as hard as she could at his arm, finally stopped him from walking, he felt a bit guilty for laughing that way in the circumstances. 'Why're you laughing?' Teresa inquired gently, but with a note of anxiety. Ntanya went on laughing, only he was a little subdued this time. Teresa repeated her question slowly again.

'Was he still capable of that?'

'Who?'

'The old man, the dead man.'

'No, not really. He fussed and fumbled a lot, you know — the way old people want to be given something hard to chew that they can't chew; they just pass it around in the mouth because they don't have any teeth. He was talking and cursing all the time about how good he was when he was young. I really wished he could have done it, well and properly, for his own sake instead of lying there talking to himself and wetting my face with his tears and runnings from the mouth. I felt sorry for him and afterwards I felt like being sick and then I washed myself all over.'

'Poor old man,' Ntanya said, 'I hope I'll never be that old.'

'I'll be there with you so that we can fuss and fumble together,' Teresa replied. They both laughed. 'Let's rest a bit?' she asked. They sat down looking at the night-setting sun without saying anything, Teresa resting her hand on Ntanya's thighs. After some time Teresa asked Ntanya without moving her eyes, addressing the setting sun rather than Ntanya, 'Are you angry because I went to bed with these men? I had to tell you. My mother taught me to tell the truth all the time. She was wonderful. She tried so hard to make me a good honest little girl, hoping that one day I'd meet a nice boy and we could be married. I guess she didn't foresee that, being ashamed of rags, I'd wind up at Maria's house. It was so nice in her days. There were no places like Maria's, and Kachawanga abounded in love and hatred. Now neither is found. Then, mothers loved their children and worshipped their husbands. Men quarrelled

67

fiercely, fought each other; but they also loved each other in a way and then — dying like the old man, without anybody to mourn you but two broken men and women. Being buried by the road like a dog. Why, a man thinks nothing of allowing his wife for a night. Today all there is is money, and a position. Why, even new-born babies are government officers. We shall soon be a country of government officers, money and propaganda. All these half-truths being dished out on the radio, all those things directed at making one believe that there's nothing left but money and guns and the police. . .'

Ntanya was looking at her all the time, rubbing her neck as if to ease the pain of her confession and her fear of what was happening. Poor child, he thought. She too is hurt. She too is starting on that bitter mapless road that he had found so fertile the night before and that he wanted so much to forget through her. He must protect her from this erosion. He must pull her back to the illusion of the flesh, for her own sake and for his own. After her confession, he could not hear clearly what she was saying. He did not want to hear anything else. He just wanted to touch her, touch her, touch her always and make her forget. If only they could touch always. He pulled her face to him and rested it on his chest as he took his turn to address her, looking at the now setting sun. 'Do you want to hear the number of women I have gone to bed with?'

'No' she replied.

'Why did you tell me then?'

'Because I am a woman. When a woman goes to bed with a man either she does it because she has been forced to in one way or another, in which case she has a hard time forgetting the humiliation, or else she goes to bed with a man because she likes him in which case a part of that man is always left in her. With you men it's different. Going to bed with a woman is just like blowing your nose.'

'You know a lot for a girl of your age,' Ntanya replied, playing with the hand that was pulling at his nose.

68

'I have suffered a lot for a girl of my age,' she replied.

'I'm not really interested in who you went to bed with. I probably couldn't remember the list of names. It's long and some of the women I never met twice. In the town it was terrible. You went to bed with a woman so that you could hurt yourself some more. It's always there; the impulse of a child who has been annoyed by its mother cutting its finger to spite its mother. Or because one had nothing else to do; it gets very lonely there. Or just because one had lost respect for mankind.'

'Were you cruel to these women?'

'Yes I think so. Most of the time I was.'

'I hope you will never be cruel to me.'

'I hope so too! Anyway I'm not interested in what you did. I'm interested in what you will do.'

'Why?'

'Because you're going to be my wife, my only wife. Because I feel about you the way I never thought it was possible to feel about a human being again. I feel blood coming back into my veins again. You've saved me. You in the way you were talking about love and hatred abounding in Kachawanga!'

'Oh Ntanya, my darling, Ntanya my husband, Ntanya my mother, a father, I will love and serve you all my days. I promise by that setting sun there. I'll love you and spoil you and raise your big fat children.'

She had weighed him down to the ground and she was running her hands over his short woolly hair, kissing his throat and chest with tears of joy, of life rediscovered, wetting his neck and chest. He surrendered himself with his arm around her repeating slowly and inaudibly, 'Yes, yes my darling.' They lay there till it was almost dark. Suddenly Ntanya got up. He had been thinking, thinking that he could not possibly expose this poor girl to another death. He must save her from that. He would take her and have her stay with James until his father got well or died. No sooner had this secret stratagem presented itself to him than he felt the urge to explain it to her openly, though he did hide the major point, his father's impending death.

Being only new-born in this kind of relationship he had not anticipated her reaction. 'But why can't we go together now? I'll stay in your grandmother's hut just like a sister until everything is finalised.'

He had no reason to offer, other than that he wanted to prepare a place for her, to clean up the hut, warn friends and his family, and maybe even arrange a party. However lovers see through each other as if they were made of glass, especially if they have suffered together and are both desperate. 'No, there must be some other reason you don't want me to go with you now. You're ashamed of me, and you want to have the time to tell a few lies about me first.' She flung herself away from him in affected anger, not really believing what she had said but using this affection to extract from him the real reason.

'All right, I might just as well tell you all. It's for your own sake I'm doing this. My father has been dying slowly. As we sit down here he may already be cold. They say that people who have done bad things in their lives die very slowly. My father didn't live his life properly. I wanted to save you from this. I wanted you to come after it was all over!'

'Oh darling, it's the first time since my mother died that anybody has ever wanted to shield me from harm. But I must refuse this protection. I must come with you now and stand by you, mourn with you, for he is now my father too. Please allow me to. When I said I would wash your feet everyday, I didn't mean with water only.'

By this time she lay on his chest again but Ntanya tore her off as he stood and said with command that was not bitter, 'No! You're going to stay at James's until the funeral and mourning are all over! I'll then send for you and we'll get properly married.' And with that he started moving east, homewards.

Teresa followed closely behind him humming softly an old

song about a man who would sit on a branch of a tree all day because he was happy and did not want anybody to mar his happiness; he would sit there till he had squandered every bit of his happiness and then go down again to wait for many years till he could accumulate enough to go back to the tree. Teresa started to improvise on this strange ditty which must have come down with the Arabs, for who else but mystic desert-dwellers would think of happiness perched on a tree. She started to sing softly about how she was going to plant her tender little tree, water it every day until it became big and that then she would call it happiness tree and climb up there every time she was happy. This made Ntanya laugh as he imagined her an old lady, for she would be old before the tree grew big enough, trotting to try to squander her sunset morsel of happiness. He was about to tell her that she could not run away with her happiness and leave him when Teresa asked, what would have happened to this man if somebody had cut down the tree? They both laughed, Ntanya replying with the carelessness of happiness 'I don't know. Maybe he would just sit there and cry and then his happiness would get wet.' They pulled each other at the waist tightly and went on laughing.

Darkness was slowly closing in but one could still see the narrow pathway that meandered in its carelessness toward the destination they were not too impatient to reach. Birds were still singing, especially the evening dove, and grasshoppers were moving around noisily in the dry grass. A few herd-boys were crying goodnight to each other across the valleys. A cow or two was mooing because of its overloaded udder or because it missed its calves which had stayed at home. Nevertheless Kachawanga was strikingly quiet this evening. Teresa was talking about how beautiful it was, with birds and grasshoppers singing their praise to God. Her voice fell on the love-full ears of Ntanya who wanted it to go on and on talking and did not care a bit about words. He just cared for the voice, the sweet-bitter sting of her voice which seemed to turn everything upside down and challenge him to explore realms of sensation and feelings he hardly suspected existed in him. She had complete control over him now; she could go on talking, move east or west, and he would follow provided this voice still scratched the empty brushland in his heart. Yes, if this heavenly voice went on watering this dry brushland that could have caught fire any time, he would follow just as if all the gods were beckoning him 'Come up, come up to the hill of Kachawanga, way up from the valleys.' Is that strange, reader, I ask you? Have you wondered at times whether there is any difference between the love of a man for a woman and his love for God? They are both founded on weakness, the only true human greatness, are they not?

When Ntanya replied that the birds, who were now singing less and less, as if they were not too grateful to God for the darkness, were probably just singing to each other, singing the little birds to sleep and extolling their lovers, he was not disagreeing with her; he was just tapping the source of this stream for more voice, for he was afraid she might stop talking. But she went on and on about how everything in life that was true and good was a praise to God, that she was not really sure what that meant, but that her mother had told her so.

When they got to James's house it was already pitch dark. Ntanya in his happiness thought James was also happy and he wanted to surprise him, having forgotten all that went on the night before. So he quietly unlatched the door, while Teresa stayed out in the darkness. James was sitting down with his head on the table and the lowered lantern wick gave the room the unreality of a beautiful sunset.

In the process of slowly closing the door, the iron latch clicked and made James start. He had been crying. 'Oh my God, not you too,' Ntanya said to himself, and then he remembered about how he had behaved the night before. '*Pole*, James, *pole*, my friend,' Ntanya said as he moved closer to him and taking his white handkerchief, the very one he had spread out before sitting on the stone the night before, he wiped his tears dry. He did not know what suffering was affecting James. Indeed just a few days before he would not have thought it possible behaviour for a government officer – and an educated man too. What difference did it make, he was wondering, as he poured James water from a glass container sitting on the floor – much much later, he was to wonder why he gave him water as if he was going to die. What kind of sorrow had visited him? Had his mother died, or had he lost his job? Or, could it even have been that he just found himself lost, alone with his cold government files and stamps. Did that not come to the same thing, tears alone in a closed room? Ntanya did not even bother to ask.

James and all government officials of his type occupy an unenviable position in Kachawanga. As he is not big enough to be heard on the radio or at one of those incessant and boring political rallies in the market square, he cannot quite hide behind pomp and prestige. On the other hand he is not quite one of the people of Kachawanga. Had he finally found himself a dangling link in the invisible chain which tied Kachawanga to the source of the print on his stamp and files? Had he used this stamp as his only authority in executing policy and measures about which he did not know much and which he did not necessarily agree with? Was he crying because he had discovered this impotence?

These thoughts were running rapidly across Ntanya's mind as he put his arm on James's shoulder. He said nothing but just sat down next to him. Teresa, as she was afraid in the darkness, had slowly opened the door and was standing looking at the two men who were unaware of her.

'Baranya, what am I going to do?' James was saying, crying almost like a child. His head was resting on the table again and this made it difficult to hear what he was saying between his sobs and the slapping noises of his wet lips moving against the wood. 'What am I going to do? I've lost my job. They say production isn't going up in my village. That people aren't growing enough maize and cotton. Why, they even say my politics –' He started crying again.

Teresa's mothering instincts were spilling over in agitation. She could no longer remain there unseen. She leaped over and put her beautiful, though dirty, hands on James's shoulders and started massaging him. For some time James thought this was Ntanya until he felt the softness of the hands and the firm breasts pushing on his back. He looked up at her and then at Ntanya. Ntanya said she was a friend. A friend she might have been, but she was also a woman, a young girl; so he dried up his tears and sat up, trying to put on that government official look that he no longer had the right to.

'It was very nice of you two to drop in to see me. Can I give you some whisky? When the letter I got yesterday was confirmed by word of mouth by my former superior this morning I wanted to kill myself. Do you see that stick over there?' They all gazed at the pin-sharp olive peg, about three feet high, which was standing in the corner. 'I stuck it in the ground and closed my eyes with the intention of running and falling on it. I tried three times but it wouldn't work. It just wouldn't.' He clasped his hands in despair. 'I was afraid. I couldn't do it. Education and being a government officer has turned me into a woman. I remember a man a few months ago. I couldn't help his starving family because my superior had ordered me not to. He said he would die rather than face the shame of watching his children die of hunger. I thought it was just a threat, but on the following day he was hanging from that tree out there, beyond both shame and honour. But I couldn't do it, Baranya, I couldn't do it! So I took all the money I had left and went to that Indian shop just south of Kachawanga and bought myself a bottle of whisky. I wanted to get drunk. I've been sitting in this room since then but I couldn't touch it. I don't know why, but I couldn't make myself drink it. I offered some to my mother. I don't want her to know that I've been sacked; it would finish her weak heart. But she said she has never drunk European liquor, and never will. Please let me offer you some of it. Maybe with you here, I'll be able to drink a little too. Please.' They nodded.

Teresa had never tasted whisky before. She winced. She did not like its bitter medicine taste, and when water was added, it tasted much like the banana sap she had once drank during the great dry season and hunger of long ago. James was now sitting on an old wooden chair that threatened to break along its many cracks every time he moved. He looked at Ntanya and then at Teresa, his portion of the bitter liquid in a cup between his hands as if he was still asking permission to drink. Evidently he was not used to whisky either, since his petty official's salary allowed him only the luxury of bottled beer. 'Come on, drink it down, Baranya,' Ntanya said. In one gulp James got the stuff down and spat the bitterness clinging in his mouth on to the cement floor while refilling his cup. 'Have some more, er? What's her name Baranya?' he said extending his generosity to Teresa.

'Teresa,' she replied and shook her head at the bottle.

'Then you'll have some more Baranya, won't you?' Baranya tilted his cup without replying. James had another cup, and yet another. The others just looked on. Teresa looking at James from the corner of her eyes while tidying up the mess of files and papers on the table. Ntanya whirled the liquid around and around his mouth before he swallowed; he watched James as if he was a child who was playing with a razor. The whisky was not without effect and James, a little cheered up, broke the silence. 'You know Baranya, you may think this is stupid, but I think life is a bloody cheat. It is, it is,' he said with emotion letting the cup with its contents break in many pieces on the floor. 'Take me for instance.' He was back in the drama club at school. 'I went to school and studied hard, thinking that one day I should come back and help my people. I wanted to be helpful to my people and honest to myself. That's the only reason I became a Christian because they told me at school that it's easier to be honest when one has religion. And I believed it. I've worked day and night on files, reports and correspondence. I talked with my people day after day about how this and that should be done. And things were going just fine. Then the government changed its policy and the people objected, but I thought this was just a temporary stress. It would pass. But you know nothing really passes. Every act just calls in another and another till one sits, like myself today, wondering where it all started.' He was now drinking from the bottle. 'I prayed and prayed and worked harder and harder. I sided with the government, thinking that I trusted in its wisdom. Whereas, as a matter of fact, I was just abdicating my judgement. Then finally that man hanged himself out there. Then I started getting nightmares. I couldn't sleep. He was looking at me in my sleep. In one nightmare he even said that I and the government would never forget him. And then he asked me who was the victor. Me or him? I'd have knelt down and prayed for forgiveness from him but my nightmare ended and I lit the lamp and wrote a letter about it to my superior. He said I was getting childish or mad and warned me that if this went on he'd take disciplinary action. I worked harder and harder but my people would no longer accept me. Correspondence from the other end became harsher and harsher. Then a week ago, I had another nightmare. The dead man asked me again who had won. When I got up again I wondered: I still wonder who won. It's probably not me, and the government doesn't suffer nightmares. I decided that though I was a government official, I was also a man with two balls dangling between my legs.' Teresa winced at this profanity. 'I decided to be what I should have been to start with: a man first, and a government official next. I wrote to my superiors and told them that the government was all wrong, that it was much more important to consider people's feelings.' He took a swig from the half-empty bottle and laughed. 'But I guess I'm now a man only and nothing else; and now that I'm a man I want to kill myself. I don't know what to do with myself. And yet I'm not man enough to kill myself. That's what I mean by saying life is a bloody cheat!'

He was taking another swig at the bottle but Ntanya took it away from him. 'Let it settle, Baranya.'

'I'm only a little girl.'

'Ha! ha! ha! You're a very big little girl,' James was laughing in his momentary salvation.

Teresa ignored the interruption, 'I'm only a little girl, but I've also suffered as an orphan, and therefore I know a thing or two. I once wanted to kill myself when a man abused me, but I decided not to. Not because I was afraid to, but because I remembered my mother's words that no matter how bad life is, it is always better than death. It's only a fool who, looking at the dry grass we have now, will throw his hands to heaven saying we're finished and in his despair kill himelf. You and I know that the day he'll be buried it will be in a wet grave. You talked about being a man. You're not man enough if you kill yourself because of something that would make a woman cry. I once gave up hope, yes, even yesterday I was shivering around my emptiness. As I looked at the sun setting yesterday I felt very much as if my life was setting with it unlived, like a chick dying before it is hatched. But today it rained in my heart and even now great streams are flowing in my heart.'

'And they'll never stop flowing again' Ntanya said putting his arms around her.

This time she did not ignore the interruption; she looked at him and put her arm around his own silently flowing streams and continued in that same serious advice-of-your-life tone without taking her eyes from James. 'If my foolishness had prevailed, I'd not have been there today to hear the birds praise God this evening. The man who killed himself might have won. But who'd have lost in your case? I tell you who: your mother, us and you! There's a sort of victory which comes out of defeat you know!'

All this time the two men were looking at her. To Ntanya it was as if he was back on the pathway walking east with her again, hearing only the voice and a few words here and there, like much-blurred images when in deep meditation. James had been sobered up by her speech and his attention magnetised. He was quite surprised by Teresa's profound and clear wisdom. Teresa was good at this. She had been playing mother, God and confessor to many ever since she was a little child. She could rehearse in her supple mind a speech that could save people; she had as a witness survived great odds. She had had her moments of trial, at which times she always gazed at the sun. Then she had simply become aloof with her secret suffering. But never had she despaired of the possibility of the sun rising again in her heart. When she imagined the light and warmth it would generate she would gaze at the solar sun and suffer convulsions of expectation.

'You two are in love,' James said without moving his eyes from Teresa who was smiling in victory.

'Yes, we're going to get married soon.'

'You are a lucky man, Baranya. It's difficult for a man to get a woman who is good and wise and at the same time a woman he won't scratch his belly with when sharing the same bed.' Teresa smiled. There was a space between her teeth which, together with her brown skin, exaggerated their whiteness in the dim light.

'Yes, it's just as she was saying, Baranya; one should never close the hope door to happiness and love. Maybe now that you've lost your job you'll have the time to search and search for yourself. Have you seen the way a lion behaves when a prey escapes it? It stares at itself. Maybe in the long run it was a good thing you lost your job. One never really knows. God works in strange ways. We're too short-sighted and impatient.'

Teresa went over and giving him a gentle shoulder massage, said, 'We'll get married and till the land. We won't get rich but we won't starve. We'll raise a family and send our children

78

to school. To hell with the government and your former superior. I see my next assignment is to get you a good girl, a healthy girl from Kachawanga, not these school urchins that you educated men talk about – girls who spend all their time licking white shoes because they have had a bit of dust on them – but a girl who can fling a hoe from sunrise to sunset, raise your children and make you happy.' She tapped him lightly on the cheek. The Tilley lamp was wavering in thirst. Teresa knew what she was talking about when she talked about making a man happy. Throwing her glance around, she noticed a bottle of paraffin oil under James's bed in the other room, and was soon busy replenishing the oil in the round silver-plated reservoir of the lamp.

After a long meditation James was saying, 'You're right Teresa. I guess what I really need is a woman to set me right and console me. We've got to find one who is like you, though.' Teresa did not really hear what he was saying, she was too busy with the pump of the lamp. Neither did she particularly want to hear. She was a good doctor and knew her treatment had worked; therefore the opinions of the patient did not count that much.

'I want her to stay here, Baranya. I want her to stay with you until all is over with me at home' Ntanya said.

'Do you trust me that much?'

'No I trust her.'

James was a bit hurt.

'You should trust him even more. You have known him longer,' Teresa the mediator put in.

'Of course I trust him, I was just joking,' Ntanya submitted.

'Sure Baranya, I'll turn that store into her bedroom. There's a wooden bed in the *dari*. I am afraid it's not very comfortable. But don't you think people will talk? But what am I saying: let them talk.'

'I'll stay in your mother's hut. Then I can help her with fetching the water, cooking and the other chores.'

'No, no, you'll make her start talking all over again about not having had another child, a daughter.'

Teresa was never to meet defeat again. 'You are wrong Baranya — can I call you Baranya too?'

'I guess women don't use men's nicknames, but I don't see why not.'

'Thank you. You're wrong, I think. I'll make her desire a daugher-in-law.'

Ntanya rushed over to her as if to jokingly say that though he might not be intelligent as she, he was more physically powerful. He picked her up gently and lowered her back to the ground again saying affectionately, 'Oh, you!'

'Okay,' James said, 'I'll take you to her and explain. She is a very understanding woman.'

'Well, till tomorrow, I'll leave you two to your own devices. I've to be getting home. They must be worried by now, those who are still living. And Baranya, I don't need to take that monstrous peg and this bottle with me, do I?'

'I may be a fool but I'm neither an idiot nor a madman. Besides, I've got friends, haven't I? I was just exhausted, that's all. And then too you've not come to see me lately, you bastard.'

'Till tomorrow, goodnight then,' Ntanya said as he shook their hands and disappeared in the darkness whistling with joy, having forgotten both his father and all that had happened to him up to that afternoon.

His father had got considerably worse that evening. Even his mother who had been so hopeful that morning showed a streak of despair as she admonished Ntanya. 'It's like the young men of today. Your father is lying here dying and yet you could go out all afternoon. During my days . . . '

'I went to a burial,' Ntanya interrupted.

'It's said that a lizard always leaves its own dying and goes to mourn for the dead of others.'

Ntanya lost his temper. 'What the hell would I have done if I was here, tell me? Could I save him if he's to go?'

'Please, please,' Onya said. 'Don't you two have any respect for such an occasion? How can you quarrel at such a place? Grandmother, you're just tired. Let's go to sleep.'

'Yes daughter. I'm probably just tired and at my age it's difficult ... ' she said as she groped her way out of the hut. Onya followed her. Ntanya could notice a coldness in Onya towards him. She had not touched him on the shoulder tonight and when she brought him his food she just left it standing on the floor and walked out without even saying goodnight.

Ntanya lay on the bed with his father next to him but not touching, since it was the only one in the hut. He could not sleep. He found himself suspended, between the night before and that evening, like a washing line between two posts. He could not reconcile these two any more than he could bring the two antipodes of a bird's egg to touch without breaking the egg. But he persisted in trying to find a link between his search for what had gone wrong and his love for this woman. And was it love? He had let the tin paraffin burner go out, though a bottle of paraffin was standing next to it; but, as if he really cared about the light, his eyes were still glued to the dying embers of the wick. As he lay he thought: 'It appears at times as if one's experiences are disconnected grains. That the man who wakes up yawning in the morning wanting to go back to bed is in fact a distant relative of the same man sweating in the fields in the hot afternoon sun or making love at night. But much as the days imperceptibly follow each other there is a link, a subterranean bond that joins these days into a period, a week, a generation or an epoch. Could there be a link between this woman I have just said I will marry and my dying father – who maybe isn't my father at all? Could this new-found ecstasy be but a reversal, a turning inside out of all my tribulation in this land, this world that has refused my handshake of friendship? Could this indeed be but asking the same question I asked at my mother's grave backwards, as I hear Arabs from the North write?' These questions were passing across the stage of his mind lightly, very lightly like bird feathers blowing in the wind, leaving no tracks behind them. He did not force them on or rush frantically pursuing them, the way he had the night before. He let them pass on slowly from the conscious world to the beautiful unconsciousness of a dream. He dreamt of Teresa. They were walking east. Teresa was in front of him. She was a big girl and he was only a little boy. There were many animal noises around in the dusk of his dream but one noise in particular interested him because it was strange and sounded like one of his playmates relaying a message. He wanted to listen, even to follow the noise, but Teresa would have none of it. 'If you go back you'll be eaten by a leopard or any one of those ravenous animals. Let's rush home before it's late.' 'But my home is not in that direction,' Ntanya objected. 'If your home is not eastwards, then you have no time home,' was Teresa's dream-reply. He listened again for a moment unafraid of the darkness or the strange voice calling, for he was but a little child in this dream and little children can play with a cobra comfortably. And then he hesitated and, Teresa being closer than the voice, followed her. She came back, held his hand and walked on with him eastwards only for a while, when looking up to her he noticed that it was not Teresa he was walking eastwards with but a strange woman. And then this strange woman melted into the air the way evil jinnis had disappeared in the stories he had once been told by his grandmother. He stood there lost, not even hearing that strange voice any more, and in this directionlessness his dream had receded into a pure memoryless sleep.

Ntanya woke up before sunrise. He did not have the time to attempt to puzzle out the meaning of this pregnant dream.

Ntanya found his father's hand was resting stiff across his chest. He was dead. He must have thrown his limbs around in his final struggle to propel himself to the ultimate peacefulness of non-existence; in the process, his right hand had finished up resting on Ntanya's chest. Ntanya did not panic, he simply bent the stiffened limb back on to the half-naked body of the dead man to give him the rigid finality that one sees in a picture of an Egyptian mummy. At times, one's mind tends to concentrate with effort on the least significant of details. One day Ntanya had seen a bride weep her brown eyes red because a fly had excreted on her calico wedding tunic. Ntanya wondered whether there was any significance in that his father's arm had been thrown over his chest rather than over his face or mouth.

It is one thing to lie at the bedside of the dying and quite another to lie at the bedside of the dead. A long time ago in Kachawanga they burnt the houses in which a person had died in order to throw away death and her spoils. They do not do so any more because houses are more expensive to build. As a result death remains there and sneaks back again.

Ntanya stood behind the hut facing east. It was still a little dark, but the red ball that was to dry so many tears in the course of the day was just over the horizon. Ntanya gazed at it saying aloud, 'You had better come up prepared today with all your house-cleaning implements. Don't forget a mop. You've a messy house waiting for you.' The sun came up slowly shaking off the hurried rising. Ntanya leaned back on the hut still facing it as though addressing an only friend. He was thinking of the burial. The process started in him by Teresa had been set on fire by the stiff hand that had rested on his chest a little while ago. Death liberates the ones who have been waiting rather than the dead; for Ntanya this death was like the painful relief a man feels when a jigger is removed from his foot. His father had ended speaking by saying 'My, my, my.' Now whatever followed 'My,' whatever his father had known, had been made to evaporate and disappear like a drop of water in a desert, by the stiff hand which had been fluttering in the darkness the night before. This is what completed Ntanya's liberation. With his father dead there was nothing left to know, nowhere to search. Like one lost and mapless in a jungle he might just as well make himself a catapult and kill birds for dinner. He must think about the funeral.

Death is a social affair in Kacha-wanga. Dying is rather like emigrating to another village, though never to come back. As with any parting there must be a farewell party and a send-off. Since the other village is everybody's ultimate destination the one who leaves cannot go disgruntled, lest he bear a grudge at the next meeting.

Ntanya continued thinking about the funeral, of how all the elders had to be informed of the mourning, and about the big party when he would have to slaughter the cow — his family's only and pregnant cow, Kibisa. He was still gazing at the risen sun. There was something wrong with this particular sunrise. It flickered at the eyes as if it was nervous and for no reason. Ntanya was saying, 'Don't, don't, everything is as it should be,' when a deafening shriek interrupted him.

His grandmother had gone into the hut and had been met by death sitting victorious over her son's remains. She had jumped out and ripped her tunic off and bellowed her message to herself across the valley. She danced round and round the shreds of her tunic, spilling her last saved store of tears and groaning in anguish. Her stomach was moving up and down, up and down as if the baby she had carried so long ago was trying to come out. She finally knelt down facing east saying softly,

'Take him, take him. You never allowed him rest. Take him; you are the hungry one. You have stolen my milk because I'm an old defenceless woman. Take him. You never knew my pain of peeling unripe bananas for the child because these breasts were dry.' She tugged at a breast with one hand and poured dust on them with the other. Ntanya was standing by her now. He knelt down next to her and helped her smear dust all over her quivering body. Now she had two hands left to pull at her breasts.

Onya took the children over to Mirisho's household, wiping the tears from her eyes with the back of her hand and once in a while saying 'Mm! Mm!'

Ntanya's youngest brother was asking, 'Where are we going?'

'You're going to stay at Mirisho's for a while. Father has gone on a trip and we're expecting many visitors.'

'Is that the reason you are crying?'

'Yes, because we don't have enough food to feed them.'

'Then we can slaughter Kibisa for them.'

'Yes, I guess we'll have to.'

The mother's cry spread out like a dry bush fire. It was the hot season. Though her son was neither the most respected nor the most loved man in Kachawanga, he had had children. People with children must be wept for in Kachawanga for they do not really die, unlike the nameless old man, since they leave themselves behind in their children. The mother's message echoed and rolled across the valley drowning the sunrise songs of the birds.

Men with scars on their faces inflicted by Ntanya's father screamed 'Mm! Mm!' in painful liberation; for a man does not really defeat his opponent in death, but only leaves the humiliation and challenge hanging forever. The 'Mm! Mm!' spread out from one early morning household to another, everybody rushing out of bed with his dreams still hanging on his eyelids saying 'Mm! Mm!' and passing it to the next household, as if it was a calabash of millet beer. The 'Mms' were drowned in the ululations of the women folk. They too might have invisible scars because of Ntanya's father, but their mourning was genuine. They were mothers and knowing what birth meant they also probably knew more about what death meant. The older mothers were the loudest in their 'Uu Uus' partly because their stomachs were emptier. Old, young and future mothers ran out one after another to witness the finished product of their deepest aspirations. Some were still naked, with their babies violently and unperturbedly sucking their breakfast. Some of the mothers, who were younger and therefore more aware of their nakedness, had thrown kangas or torn blankets over their shoulders. They danced to and fro in broken rhythms, a few steps in front and one back again and again, but advancing forward as if they were soldiers of many age-groups united against the unseen enemy, proclaiming that though he had taken one captive he had not touched the front line. Among the throng of soldiers was Teresa who followed on rubbing her sleep out of her eyes in her impatience with this slow to and fro advancement.

The children violently torn away from sleep were gazing at the men and women open-mouthed, though not with excitement but with boredom. This had been repeated too many times in Kachawanga. Always the same thing happened; some woman would bleat like sheep and then the whole village would stampede. Yet the children would not be allowed to leave their compounds, and they had not even been told what the uproar was all about. The sun was slowly bathing Kachawanga in light, but it was not warm as yet. So the children shook their heads and went back to the huts either to sleep undisturbed or to stick their feet in the cold ashes in the hearths scratching their stomachs in remembrance of yesterday's supper and warmth.

The men followed behind the women. Friends were in front, with bitter masculine tears weighing down their eyelids and moustaches, spitting out the bitterness of the stale night snuff.

86

Enemies and the indifferent followed, saying again and again, 'Mm Mm' as if to inflict the stomach punch they had dreamt about so many times. Slowly the women advanced to and fro with Teresa squashed in between trying to shoot out, to escape from this too slow movement, to run to her lover. James too was trying to press his way through the throng of men with one hand while the other tied his trousers. Both were closed in like individual ants in a column, swaying to and fro with the rest of the crowd that was moving unhurriedly with practised deliberation. The men were now singing the death acceptance song, known by all who had been initiated in Kachawanga, with the accompaniment of the women's 'Eee.'

Men: Someone told me my brother's house was on fire.
Women: Ee-Ee . . .
Men: What do we do when our brother's house is on fire?
Women: We run to help.
Men: But there is no water to put out the fire.
Women: Ee . . . Ee . . .
Men: What do we do when brother's house is on fire and we don't have any water?
Men and women: We cry with him and put out the fire with our tears.

They repeated this and other lamentations over and over again while strangers and strayed urchins improvised the words or just murmured the tunes; for there were many idlers who out of boredom would rush behind such a procession, invariably out of step. Teresa was slowly squeezing her way past people, following neither the rhythm of the songs nor the steps. James had been caught in the men's rhythm, and was moving to and fro in tune, saying the words and not singing them. He had known the song for a long time but had not thought about the words.

By the time they reached the white-ant partition of the dead man's household Teresa had freed herself from the rest of the women. She had dashed out and knelt by Ntanya, who was seated holding his grandmother on his lap. Onya was brushing off the dust and ashes on the shaking old woman's nose and eyelids. Glances of suspicion and reproach were exchanged between the three of them. The mother was not, however, aware that the person who was dusting her right side was not her own kin as was the custom.

Soon it was the mother and her children, and not the dead man inside the hut, who were surrounded by a large part of the adult population of Kachawanga. The silent crowd stood in front and the younger ones behind. They let the relations weep first, for one weeps most in company. Not a movement could be seen in this solemn congregation. There was only the sound of the squealing of the mother and her daughters. Occasionally there would be an outburst by a woman overcome by emotion either because of a powerful memory of an event in the life of the dead man or because she was thinking of her own children or her impending old age. The crowd would then make way for her and some would follow her out of the circle to help to console her or help her pour dust over her torso. Most of the men simply stood biting their lips or hanging their heads; a few close relations and friends dropped a tear or two on the thirsty ground; some ran from the nose and mouth.

The sun had risen so high in the sky that a man's shadow to the west was only as long as himself. By this time the urchins and strangers had become bored and had either scattered or sat down in the sun waiting for the party. Miila was the elder of Kachawanga; he deserved the title, not only because he had the record of doing the least stupid or cowardly things in the village, but also because one could count all the bones on a body that had little else. He should have the right to be the master of ceremonies for such an affair.

He moved forward towards the mother and after clearing his throat, repeated what he had said over a million times on other similar occasions. 'Elderly mother of children, you have wept your share. Leave the rest to us, for an old bamboo doesn't have much sap. Some weeping washes away the gravity of our condition. But as those who have gone before told us, too much weeping disturbs their rest and washes to dust our blessings. We must shed tears with one eye and look at our blessings with the other. Nterenya did not die, he is here with us in those that are drying your tears and wiping away the bitter ashes and dust on your face. He is only across the valley on the other side where the sun warms him. At every sunset, which is his sunrise, he looks across at us. There they have a chance to start over again. You'll be surprised when you and I go across; we may find him a chief there beyond night and day. You can see the sun is always red when it is leaving them or joining them, relaying the message to us again and again that they are happy. So good mother don't weep any more. And children, don't weep any more for where are we all going. A man with many children sells his land with pain.' Miila then took the old woman in his arms to the shade for it was now getting hot. The daughters and other female relations, strongly weighed down in their hearts, followed behind with Onya carrying a gourd of water. The crowd disappeared one after another with the older women crouching once in a while to smear themselves with dust, and the babies starting to cry because they had been ignored for so long. The younger men stayed behind. There was work for them.

Far from being particularly sad, Ntanya felt only the weight of the new responsibility that had been thrust on his shoulders, the grave and heavy responsibility of becoming the head of a family for whose beginning he had not been responsible.

As it was customary, however, he had to put on a grave air. As people went away, Ntanya, Mugia and James and Miila withdrew behind the hut to the very spot where Natanya had been standing gazing at the sun, planning the events of the day. The man was to be buried when the shadows slanted east as much as they slanted west. And Kibisa, the family's only cow, was to be exchanged for Miila's bull and slaughtered before sunset.

James offered to buy the necessary drums of millet beer. The committee's deliberations were swift and Ntanya was hardly required even to give opinions. They walked off and told the waiting young men of the plans. They scattered, saying that they would come back at an agreed length of their shadows.

Ntanya wandered back to the mourning women who were now quiet with exhaustion. He noticed that Teresa was not there, but thought that she might have gone to relieve herself. The mother recognised his hand when he ran it across her face. 'Is everything as it should be, my husband?' Every woman, even suckling baby girls, has to have a husband in Kachawanga. It is a manner of speech. Her husband had died long ago and then her son had become her husband and now that he was dead her grandson was her husband; for a woman whose womb is blessed with menfolk is never widowed as long as they live.

'Everything is as it should be, mother of people.' Ntanya went back to Miila and others who had started the day's bitter work inside the hut. Before Ntanya and his central committee had moved to the east of the hut an idea had come to Teresa who was never too sad to be practical. She remembered that nowadays people who could afford it were buried in wooden boxes rather than in their blankets or tunics. She had left with hardly a word, and had run swiftly to Maria's house. She remembered that Maria had not given her the share of the money she had earned from the man who had abused her. She thought that if she went there now Maria would give it to her. She would buy some timber and take it to James so that Ntanya would not even know. For a short while she had qualms about using money that had bitterness in it for such a purpose but then she told herself that this death too had bitterness in it, and that there is nothing wrong in mixing bitterness with bitterness.

When she got to Maria's house she found the door closed. She knocked a couple of times and, despairing of Maria's being there, turned back in confusion and disappointment. On her way back a car pulled up on the dirty road bathing her in dust. It was the same man who had abused her in Maria's house and given more money for doing so than she had ever seen. She felt like vomiting but since there was nothing in her stomach to vomit she just hiccupped.

'I didn't pay you enough last time.'

'Hic-'

'You were quite good you know, only you should clean yourself more, and stay away from all those barefoot paupers.'

'cup'.

'Maybe next time I'll buy you a beautiful dress like the European women wear and perfumed soap, then if any one of those sisal-cutters touches you, I'll shoot them.'

'Hic-'

'I'll be back tonight. Here buy some soap and wash up, eeh!'

'Hic-'

He thrust a twenty shilling note in between her breasts and drove off. Teresa felt she was going to faint. In the cloud of dust which enclosed her, Teresa sat down on the scorching dust crying and beating the scorching ground over and over again. It was as if she had turned into a physical monster and she was crushing this vulgar and pompous creature, car and all.

It was hot now. The sun was a ball of white fire one could not look at; not a speck of cloud was to be seen in the surrounding ocean of blue. Teresa dragged herself up slowly like a snake with a broken backbone. In the process, the blue money fell to the ground. She felt ages old and wished that she had a mirror to look at her face. She walked a few steps, stopped for a while and turned back to the money. She looked at it and then turned around to the west and looking at the horizon where the azure blue of the sky met the smoky blue of the western hills and turned into the dry brown which surrounded her dress, her body, everything except the blue bill, she threw her head and her arms up towards the sun saying, 'What have I done? Have I killed your son?' She bent down, and after shaking her head at the bill picked it up and tucked it back where the donor had placed it.

The carpentry shop was at the southern end of the village where the southern flanks of the hills surrounding Kachawanga turned their backs to the rest of the world. It was a small tin-roofed shed laden with timber of many varieties. Some was second-hand and coated with mud, having been taken from some dismantled houses in other villages to the south; some was ant-eaten and still wet with the white ants at their noon meal; other planks were still wet with sap, having been freshly cut. When Teresa approached the carpenter was sitting on an unfinished stool having lunch with his assistants from a common platter and a large wooden bowl. His left hand was suspended in mid-air holding a ball of ugali dripping with the yellow curry-laden white-ant sauce.

The carpenter was a middle-aged man with hair straying haphazardly on to his unshaven face. He had big fleshy lips which curled up like the snout of a pig. He wore a loin-cloth and an unbuttoned shirt exposed his well-rounded muscles of the chest and arms, which were a mark of his profession.

'Peace be to you, our sweetheart.'

'Peace be to you, my fiancee.'

'I can say the man whose bride is looking for a wedding box is not unlucky.' The assistants laughed. This was always the second sentence the carpenter addressed to his women customers. Teresa did not reply to the irony. 'A workman's place is his home, and as our people believed from long ago, if one enters a man's house without sharing the meal on the table, the house won't eat again,' he said, motioning towards the family table. The assistants grudgingly made way for Teresa. She sat down on the ground and with her dirty fingers started rolling a ball of ugali until it was a perfect sphere, then with her thumb she bored a hole in it and dipped it into the small amount of sauce in the bowl. She started to nibble at it unwillingly. She had not eaten at all that day but she was not hungry. 'I understand our sweetheart. When one is excited especially just before marriage one's stomach moves up and down so much it can't take anything.' The carpenter was laughing. 'He is handsome and rich, this young man of yours, isn't he?' He did not give her time to answer. 'He should be. Why you see these pot-bellies of mine here. They're all my sons. You know they inherited their father through and through. I'm not handsome.' This was an understatement. 'And I'm not particularly intelligent. But in my days there were no schools or I might have been an officer – why, I've seen some pretty stupid ones. Yes, what was I saying? Well, if any of these ant-eating pot-bellies down there had been handsome and rich rather then depending on their poor father, why, I'd have married them to an elegant lady like you; then I'd have been proud to be called her father-in-law. As it is they will wind up marrying an ugly woman like their mother and then their children will be worse than them. One can't keep a straight line for a long time you know, not even when cutting timber; the line bends one way or another. Our family line has been bending for a long time now.' He started laughing. Teresa was not listening.

The youngest of the assistants, a boy of barely twelve said, 'Our father, I don't think that's very funny.'

'It's because your head is made of wood; that's why you never see anything that's funny.' The other assistants laughed. 'Tell me about this man of yours, our sweetheart.'

Teresa, who had not said a word so far, replied coldly, 'I'm looking for timber to make a box to bury his father in.' Some of the assistants let their balls of ugali fall back to the platter, others opened their mouths as crocodiles do and let the moist food drip out at the corner while the carpenter hung his head. 'I'm sorry, my daughter. My wife always told me that my mouth was too big. Instead of getting some thread to sew it up I always replied that her rump too was too big. But then one never knows what to say to a stranger or to anybody for that matter. One takes a risk, and at times one might wind up joking about birth rites to a woman with stomach tumours. I once did. I am so sorry.'

'You've done no wrong.' Teresa was feeling sorry for him. The way he talked about his wife in the past tense meant he must have lost her and, though he might not have told his assistants, he must be missing this rump now.

He held her hand and led her to the other side of the un-finished furniture piled at the corner. Teresa's eye was caught by a pile of cloth-boxes piled high one upon another in order from small to big ones until the last one was a trunk as big as a room; all of them had a crude inscription in charcoal which the youngest assistant following behind them while drying his mouth with his hands interpreted as reading, 'I am sorry'. Below it and in the same crude hand-writing was 'Reject'. She asked the carpenter what it was all about. The carpenter explained that there was a young man across the river who had refused to buy his bride-to-be a cloth-box. The girl had left him and gone off to marry an elderly man who had bought her a box. Then the young man had got the carpenter to build cloth-boxes, each one bigger than the other. He sent them to this woman to apologise, but she sent them all back. The carpenter's youngest son had found it funny to inscribe the apology on it which the woman could not read; when a box came back he would slump on it and write 'Reject'. The old man finished by saying, 'I don't know how long this is going to go on. He says I'll have to go on building bigger and bigger boxes till the last one is so big that he'll kill the woman, hus-

94

band and all and stick them in with all they owned and then stand on it and yell "I am sorry" and kill himself. I think he is just joking but one never knows. Strange things happen.'

'Yes, they do,' Teresa said. 'I don't have enough money for the box but I'll plant enough beans this coming season if you give me one season to pay.'

The carpenter replied, 'You must think me an awful person. In our days women should never have to worry as to how their in-laws are buried. But the world is walking on its ears now. No, you will accompany my children who will deliver the box free of charge. I'm a father, and a young she-impala doesn't disturb a mother licking the ears of her new-born.'

When Teresa was crossing the river, walking heavily behind the young men carrying the coffin she felt something hard nestling in her bosom. She had forgotten the pound note that lay between her breasts. She took it out and dropped it into the muddy stream and walked on quietly behind the men with her head slightly bent. People whom they came across on the road cleared off into the bush or shook their heads in sympathy.

B efore she got to the hut enclosure Teresa heard noises to her right. She turned towards their source; the boys carrying the coffin followed behind her with their heavy load and sweat on their faces. A box lay on the ground next to a large and deep hole in the ground. Her eyes met Ntanya's. He was bending down with a banana leaf in his hand to protect his grandmother from the hot sun. She noticed that he had been crying. He walked over slowly, after handing the banana leaf to James, and looked at her as if he had never seen her before. He then turned around to help the young men who stood embarrassed with the unbeautiful load. There were murmurs in the little crowd of relations surrounding the hole in the ground. Their eyes, up to then, had been fixed either on the grandmother or on the box, whose contents had come out of her so long ago. They now turned to look at Teresa. Without exchanging a word Teresa and Ntanya's eyes met again. They touched. She walked heavily to the grandmother and taking the banana leaf from James she knelt by her and protected her from the violent sun. The boys who had delivered the box scattered into the crowd of relations around the hole.

It was hot now though a man's shadow was already longer than himself. Kachawanga was dead silent as if the whole village was out surrounding the hole in the ground. Miila was supposed to have come back when his shadow was as long as himself but he had not done so. Onya had been sent to enquire whether somebody was also digging a hole in the ground for him, though this could not be since nobody had yet heard cries. She too had not come back. There was anxiety on people's faces as some got tired of standing and sat on the fresh cool soil which had been thrown up from down below. The mother sat like a slab of stone without saying anything. Even when the scorching sun moved slowly and sat on her shoulders and legs she did not move back to the banana leaf shadow. Whoever was holding the shadow had to move instead. Three times she had been offered cold millet beer from a gourd but she would have none of it. Her nephew came again with the gourd; the mother raised her unseeing eyes but did not as much as shake her head. Teresa took the gourd with one hand and tilting it, touched the old soul's lips. The mother swallowed and to everybody's surprise she did the same for Teresa. Teresa swallowed too and returned to her position.

'What if Miila wasn't coming?' Ntanya was thinking. 'Who would say the last things to be said?' These thoughts had hardly gone to sleep when muted sighs of relief were heard as two young men came carrying Miila, followed by Onya with three black drinking horns. Onya stuck one horn in her grandmother's lap and handed the others to Ntanya, who took them without looking. She went back to where her grandmother and Teresa sat and, kneeling on the other side, helped Teresa hold the leaf as if it were very heavy.

Miila, supported by the two young men was whispering something to Ntanya. He had apparently nearly broken his leg by falling in a ditch on the way back. After this he had limped on until he fell exhausted by the wayside where Onya had found him with the three horns. The two young men had been passing and lifted him up.

Since he could not stand a stool was provided and he sat down facing the fierce sun, next to the three wooden barrels of frothing beer. 'Mother of children, children of Kachawanga whose empty stomachs are today filled with bitter tears, we're assembled here with our hands empty, looking with one eye at the hole in the ground and the other at this blinding sun. We have cried all we can but you all know that there is a crying which is deeper, the cry of silence. Let us take heed and cry in silence only with half our heart; for whoever hits his head against a stone finishes up by not breaking the stone but his head. If it was possible we would all pull back the man sleeping there from the village of beyond, back to us. But it is not possible. If it was possible we would stop ourselves from getting old. But as things are, nobody sits up to cry all day because his teeth are falling out. He accepts it.'

Miila talked on and on, looking to his left and right to see whether his consolation was being received; every now and again he knitted his face with the pain of his sprained ankle. The audience sat there looking at him coldly, even with a certain amount of hostility especially when, as usual, he started recalling the dead man's history, sprinkling salt and pepper and even curry here and there. He thought that if a man had done wrong one could not tell lies at his grave. So he searched his mind to find something nice, any little thing, that was true about the dead man. He was normally never caught unaware like this, but his own pain from the left leg had prevented his thinking of the right thing to say. As he looked around, pretending to pause because of his pain and sorrow, he could see only the scars on the men's faces magnified over and over again. He closed his eyes and started softly, 'One day it was raining heavily. There was lightning and thunder and the man who is resting now there listening to us, seeing a little child walking by a tree ran out there to pluck the child from a possible death, risking his own life. This is the kind of man we have lost, O mother of children, a man with courage and goodness.' This proved to be disastrous; people around the hole started to whisper to themselves as if they had been expecting a feast at a chief's compound; they had been given nothing but a ripe banana each and in disappointment they were saying, 'Is that all?' 'Is that all?' Miila almost said aloud, 'Damn it all, I was not sharing his life with him,' but he only concluded hastily: 'Therefore . . . [Damn this custom of summing up one's history before the people, Ntanya was now thinking in sympathy with Miila] . . . Let him then, my brother, go on to his new home of adoption across the valley. And let's all go home knowing that it all is as should be.'

Ntanya's heart was beating with fury and bitterness. The feelings of the dark night after he had met Teresa were returning and knocking incessantly at his heart so hard that it seemed as if it might give way. Messy necklaces of great beads were collecting on his face, chest and arms, and his clothes stuck on him. They were not beads of sweat caused by the heat; they were too furious and big for that. They were pumped from a deep pit in the dirty reservoir of his heart, sweat beads of hatred and bitterness. His lips kept moving as he trembled. He had never hated anybody so much before. He did not even think this was possible. Up to now he had always remained with the hope that one day his father and he would make things up, adjusting themselves to the world. One day he would find out the truth of his father's condition or some evidence which favoured him. Ntanya's hatred was not final. He had always hoped that one day his father would have come and called him, 'My son let us sit down and talk. My son I've behaved this way because I've a stone in my liver.' Or, 'There was a noise which came out of my brain which I didn't understand and that is why I behaved in that way.' He would have washed his father's feet with tears and would have had a party of apology and explanation for all those people with scars. He would have sacrificed a black lamb to appease his mother. But, no, his father was lying there dead. 'Bloody cheat,' he was swearing in his thoughts looking at the coffin while mopping off his sweat with his fingers. 'You make your mess and sneak off like that leaving me and your own mother sitting here in this humiliation. While a man with a scar from you on his belly sits there with trembling lips, babbling like a child or an idiot, trying to whitewash the smelling shit you spilled on the face of the earth. Well, you haven't won, for where are you going but into the earth you've smeared shit on? Where is your strength? But he knew, and this is probably what agitated him most, that his father would have won if there had been a fight, for his father had concluded his battle lying in the box. He was fighting no more, but his memory would be there always to wrestle with Ntanya.

He felt greatly humiliated as the old man, Miila groped further and further into the darkness of his father's finished existence without finding one strand to hand on, one act to finish the sentence, 'Mother of children, and friends, here lies a man who . . .'

As Miila ended with, 'All is as it should be,' Ntanya almost cleared his throat to tell the audience what his father really was to his children, wife, mother and the world. He almost wanted to say, 'Let us reserve this honoured ceremony for men who stood with something stiff in between their legs and women

99

E

who held their nursing babies close to their breasts in the darkness. Let's throw him in the bush like a dog for hyaenas to eat.' But something, maybe his own dark fury, prevented him.

Dark and mysterious clouds were quickly being blown across the sky, but the shade only made it hotter. As was customary, Onya ripped off the upper part of her dress, smeared herself with the fresh soil from the hole and then took the horns and filled them up, one from each of the vessels. She handed the first to her grandmother, the next to Ntanya and the last to Miila.

The tired mother did not sip as was customary but quenched her thirst and handed the horn around. When the last person to wet his lips on this horn had brought it back, Teresa and Onya had to help her to the grave into which she threw the horn and contents and came back to where she was sitting before, supported by the strong shoulders of the young women. Miila threw his horn in. So did Ntanya though he just tilted the horn without touching the stuff inside and when his turn came to throw it into the grave he also dropped in some of his tears thinking that the hole was not deep enough.

Miila moved his stool closer to the grave without getting up and said, 'Now we have eaten together.' And he threw a piece of Kibisa's roast meat in though nobody had touched the meat. He then sprinkled a few drops of the beer in and again said, 'Now we have drunk together.'

Maybe because of the rain, the coffin was lowered without ceremony into the ground by the young men as soon as Miila finished. As the body went lower and lower nobody sent up a cry. Even the exhausted mother only clutched with her nails deeper and deeper into the soft soil and shook her head when she heard the thud of the coffin touching the bottom. Ntanya then rolled a stone onto the grave, and planted a marking twig which he had cut in such a way that it would not grow.

It was now raining heavily. Even before the ceremony

finished, some people had run for cover under the trees and into the family's huts. Ntanya did not seem to be in a hurry to get away from the rain. He walked slowly and deliberately, letting the mixture of the rain and sweat soak his clothes and retard his heart-beats. As he walked away, the crowd felt a kind of relief.

Big drops of rain were starting to fall and there was thunder in the east causing more whispering. The sun could still be seen shining far from the village, but Kachawanga, except for the southern corner, was covered by large black clouds.

Days had rolled on slowly, one into the other, like the weaving of a basket. Soon the long rains were really there. Wives could be seen early in the mornings wrestling blessing from the brown sticky soil, with the men either supervising their children and their wives or building hedges of thorn around the clearings. All over Kachawanga one could see only the patches of brown grinning earth surrounded by smoking weeds. Soon there would be green all over the land; even on Ntanya's father's grave a few weeds would be seen struggling upwards.

Only one patch of Kachawanga remained dry-grass yellow, and that was Ntanya's household's plot, for he had now taken the family title. After the funeral the family had moved in like bees moving into a new hive. They had not been visited in their bitter mourning save by Teresa and James. They drew into themselves, limiting family conversations to an essential minimum and not talking to people in the outside world. The children shrunk up more and more with time, since the gravity of the situation required that they should not play and since, with Kibisa dead, they could not escape in searching for green grass for her. Onya moved around absent-mindedly repeating, 'Ah! ah!' whenever somebody said something to her, and even the gloss and colour was fading under her skin.

The one most hit by this ostracism was Ntanya. Since he had to worry about the whole family's future, he had also had to carry most of their suffering. The brightness that had returned with his encounter with Teresa, the free carelessness with which he had ignored his condition and which had made him whistle in his sleep, disappeared slowly and left him sleeping for most of the day, face down on the very bed on which his father had died. Or he would sit in the sun or rain playing with the soil or mud. He felt most strongly the betrayal by the people of Kachawanga; as he realised that even those people who came to the funeral must have been mocking him in his plight. He felt even more strongly the sting of Miila, who did not even bother to pay the traditional next morning's visit, as if he had only said the last things at the funeral of a dog or a donkey. As Ntanya stretched himself in the sun, watching the smoke of burning weeds go up into the blue but wet sky, his heart sank even lower. What was he going to do with these mouths to feed when the mourning was supposed to last another two weeks and the planting week was already here? Would he go out and start clearing the land and add another abomination by working while in the period of mourning? It was not the fear of dishonouring his dead father. If this was the case he would gladly have worked from sunrise to sunset the day after the funeral. It is also true however, that with the people of Kacha-wanga turning against him in this way he was no longer quite sure. He was afraid of giving the people of Kachawanga another ball of shit to fling at him and the family. As it was, it was only the pitiful disgrace of a family disgraced by its father. As it was, he could sit there and see people walk by and looking at the fallow land shake their heads with pity though, granted, it was malicious pity. If he had as much as put matchet or a hoe on his shoulder they would both have shaken their heads and pointed fingers saying, 'Like son, like father.'

Something else troubled him even more. He remembered at the grave of his father, as he poured in the beer and his sweat, an echo, (or was it only his thoughts in anticipation?) saying, 'I'm still here. We're not through yet.' It was difficult enough to battle with an unseen opponent; that is why people are so afraid of evil spirits and jinnis that speak to you or strike an unseen blow. But now the whole village was also fighting maybe without knowing on the side of his father when he had no strength left, and could only sit there like a dying zebra letting a lion disembowel him.

Ntanya had not resolved this conflict when Onya came running and sat down next to him, panting, with a worried look on her face. Ntanya thought of his grandmother. 'What is it, Onya?' he said standing up.

'Well, Teresa—' she stopped for breath.

'No! No!' Ntanya was saying. 'She is cultivating our maize plot.' Ntanya sighed with relief.

'Well I'll go and see her.'

Ntanya hid behind a little bush and peered at her. Except for a tunic tied round her waist she had nothing on. She seemed like a machine with a well-oiled joint in her middle as she wrestled with the soil in steady cultivated blows. With a straight thrust she would bring off a chunk of the brown soil and, swinging her hoe to the left and then to the right, keep her four steps strip going all at the same time. Slowly, bit by bit, as if a mole was making a furrow through the darkness of the underground, the yellow of dry grass was yielding unwillingly to her violent thrusts and blows. Slowly the earth was shaking hands with her as she violently wrung a promise from it. Her torso was drenched in sweat and on her legs the sweat-soil mixture had caked up so that one might think that her legs were but an upward extension of the brown earth.

She must have done the job of four women. Though her

shadow was by then twice her height, she was still flinging the hoe as if she had just started, much like an old man flicking a fly-whisk for pleasure. Ntanya was touched by the fluidity that pervaded all her muscles, the way she stretched, bent and moved her arms and legs as if she was just a leaf blowing in the wind. He was overcome by the radiant fire which seemed to burn brightly somewhere inside her, the smile that played on her lips, the baby's gloss and colour that had returned to her face after so many events and suffering. Was it possible that one who was shaking before the setting sun a few days before could be so happy, so changed? Ntanya felt that he was somehow connected with this revival. His heart throbbed with victory and pleasure at this potency in him. He was still puzzled as to how one who has so little could bestow so much upon another. 'But then, a mosquito is a small insect, but it causes lethal malaria, doesn't it?' he thought as he struck with his palm at a mosquito. The noise startled Teresa.

Teresa yelled in her half-nakedness and flung her hoe to the side. She ran to cover herself with her kanga which was lying in a heap with her khaki blouse. She went up to Ntanya, looking down in her new-found maiden shyness like a small goat moving to a sacrificial pyre.

Ntanya had forgotten that he was still in mourning and was laughing while looking at her bent supple neck as she approached. When she got near to him he took from round his neck the kerchief which had become practically part of him, and wiped off the brown sweat on her neck and face, gently. He was still laughing.

'You should announce yourself when coming, I could've thrown a stone,' Teresa said.

'I did by slapping my face. In any case there is no stone here,' Ntanya replied in the breath of his laugh.

'No, there're only mosquitoes,' Teresa replied. Ntanya pulled down his face and put on an air of seriousness which Teresa mistook for a remembrance of mourning etiquette.

'What're you doing?' Ntanya asked.

She understood what he meant. And with her hand on her stomach she said softly looking down, 'This womb isn't dry, and we can cultivate only once a year. If you and the people in your household don't have mouths to feed, I do, and as I've said it's not emptiness I feed in here.' Her hand was still on her womb. She looked away from him towards the tiny baldness that she had created on the face of the earth, which appeared so large to her now. Ntanya too looked in the same direction and, without touching or exchanging a word, they both looked at the light playing on the white roots and the mica crystals like little fireflies in bright moonshine. They looked beyond at the many brown patches and the smoke rising from the land. Teresa glanced at Ntanya again quickly as if she had seen a bit of food left on his lips, and then her eyes went back to the land. She sighed from deep down in victory and relief as she noticed that there was no bitterness curling on Ntanya's lips. As she wiped the sweat on her brow there was great joy in her.

'How am I going to explain this?' Ntanya asked quickly as if addressing himself. Teresa did not reply. She went back to her patch throwing off her kanga as if Ntanya was no longer there. Her half-nakedness didn't matter any more. She hoed again. Ntanya looked at her for a while but did not see her. Bits of mica and white roots reflected the hot afternoon sun too strongly towards him; it was now behind Teresa. Ntanya could not focus her image. Shaking his head, he started back.

There was great tiredness in his legs as he moved. When he got back he sat down heavily next to his grandmother, raising a cloud of dust. His grandmother was not aware of the tears streaming from Ntanya's eyes. Ntanya was not aware of her complaint, maybe because he'd heard it so many times. She was saying feebly with trembling lips, 'I swear the sun of nowadays is just like the moon. There's no warmth in it.' Rubbing off the sweat and tears on his face, Ntanya said mechanically and casually the way he had millions of times before, 'Yes, it is.' Then he moved to the shade of the tree away from the hot sun.

There was a worried look on Onya's face as she handed to the old one a bowl of hot mashed bananas and meat. Her eyes were fixed on Ntanya who had his head between his thighs and was making his figures on the dusty ground with a finger. She was hardly paying attention to her grandmother's complaints. 'Is the food hot today, my daughter? There was so little meat yesterday.' Onya directed the old woman's hand to the wooden spoon without replying. She took to Ntanya the small bowl with a spoon in it, an aluminium spoon that had a broken handle. When he raised his head Onya noticed that there was a wetness on his eyelids and understood what had gone on. She bent down and rubbed his shoulders the way she had started to do when the other girl had come in between her and Ntanya.

Onya had not disliked Teresa. The two girls had in fact got on well. Teresa was, in a way, one of them having suffered the same tribulation of an incomplete family with its accompanying loneliness and the disgraces of poverty. Also Onya thought that now that Ntanya had found a lover she would in time be free to get married herself. She had looked at her future freedom with apprehension wondering whether any other woman, especially women of today, would be able to take care of her family the way she had, knowing herself too well how thankless and tedious a job it was. These doubts were dispelled as soon as she had met Teresa. She saw in her a woman of constant and steady temperament and purpose. Besides, she had told herself at the same time, she could not have always lived there for a woman is only a visitor in the house of her father. Something new had been stirring in her for a long time now. Every time she had seen a well-built man like Mugia she would sit under the tree and her thoughts would be far away. There seemed to be an agitation which made her restless inside. Her loins and lips would vibrate and shake. But she did not quite know what the feeling was. It was not at one point, like an itch or a mosquito bite; it was a generalised restlessness, more of a feeling of being incomplete, unfulfilled, like a bride without a bead necklace round her neck. Somehow she felt there was a yearning deep in her that she did not understand but which she believed a man like Mugia could satisfy. As she sat in the fullness of her desire rubbing her bosom and pursing her full lips she loved Teresa very much, seeing in her a vehicle towards her own fulfilment. When she had called her 'my sister', it had been with a deeper feeling than she would have used in addressing her own sister.

In spite of all this, her love for Teresa had not been without a grain of hatred and suspicion. At times, she had even felt outright though unexpressed hostility, especially when Teresa behaved as if she had more right to Ntanya than herself. One day, for instance, a few days after the funeral, Ntanya had not liked Onya's banana stew and Teresa had rushed to boil it again and add a little more coconut oil and salt. This had greatly hurt Onya who had simply gone off to listen, without hearing, the incessant and stereotyped complaints of her grandmother.

For Onya saw in Teresa not only her stepping-stone to the unknown realm of freedom from her faimly and the curse of spinsterhood, but she also saw her as a competitor for the devotion and attention of her brother Ntanya. This created a difficult problem for her, for she loved her brother very much more than she thought she could ever love any other man.

Still rubbing Ntanya's shoulders, she was whispering to him softly so that the old soul could not hear, for one thing that had faithfully remained with the old mother through her troubled age was her power of hearing. For she was always complaining about a mouse singing somewhere which nobody else could hear, but which the young ones would chase into the grass walls of the hut in the direction the old one pointed at. Onya whispered, 'We can't let this go on, surely Ntanya.

They are laughing at us enough as it is. You must stop her, even if it means our starving to death next year. Dying in disgrace can never be compensated for. Have you forgotten the look on people's faces as father went underground? I guess he too, wherever he might be, can never forget the sneer on the curled lips and the mockery in their sympathy. If he could have had a second chance, he too would have sacrificed anything to have ended neatly this affair of living by deserving a proper human funeral. No, you must stop her. Only two weeks are left. Who knows what God has got up there this year? It might rain two weeks late this year, it has before. And besides, or maybe most important of all, if grandmother hears of it, you know she'll die. You know, in spite of all her bickering, she is still very sensitive. She has still got a deep sense of self-respect and honour that has been brought almost to the breaking point. I want you to know this. Yesterday very late at night she got up thinking that I and the children were asleep. She felt her way slowly to the corner where she keeps the cowrie that she was given by her mother. It was dark and I couldn't see her, but I guess she must have held it in her hands while kneeling. She said out aloud, 'God, I didn't know it would end this way. Please end it now, I'm tired.' I heard that with my two ears. She then went back to bed, but she did not sleep because I heard her scratching her stomach much later. For her sake, Ntanya, stop her. It is not up to us to end it for her. Let's dare somebody else . . .' She was interrupted by her grandmother.

'What's that noise I hear, Onya? Have the children finished their meal already?'

Onya said, 'Yes, mother,' without taking her eyes from Ntanya.

Ntanya had been looking at the horizon all the time while Onya had been whispering to him, much as if the breeze that was now making the afternoon heat more bearable was what actually brought the message. He quickly turned his head and looked at Onya. He wanted to say something but instead his mouth closed again. He stretched his arm and slowly ran his hand over the back of her neck to and fro. Onya was still rubbing his shoulders. As they touched and looked at each other, Onya's fears evaporated. She could share Ntanya with Teresa. When Ntanya whispered to her to send some food to Teresa, she went with light feet, after refilling both Ntanya's and the old one's bowls.

Ntanya moved over and sat next to his grandmother. Tilting her bowl for her, he directed the old woman's spoon to the little food in the tilted corner. When her second bowl was finished and the old one was with the unsteadiness of old age still clanking the sides of the bowl, Ntanya poured into her bowl half of the contents of his second bowl. When the old one finally came up with a full spoon she laughed saying, 'I guess my hands are unsteady. I was scooping up at the wrong place. But it is your fault. You were directing me.'

Ntanya said, 'I was just teasing you, mother of people.'

She laughed again, saying lightly, 'It's not fair to tease an old woman who can't see.' Her hand searched in the darkness of her eyes for Ntanya's nose which she had pulled long ago when he was a boy and had teased her. Ntanya offered his nose to her straying hand and she pulled it laughing. He did not feel like being teased, but she was walking out of the heaviness of mourning.

When the old one had more than satisfied her hunger she thanked Ntanya, and Onya whom she thought was there, and lay back on her blanket. She started to complain about the sun. Ntanya went back to his former position and watched her slowly go to sleep facing the sun.

That evening, James came along and told Ntanya that there was some important business for them to discuss. The two men walked across the valley to James's home. On their way they did not say much. They both were taciturn by nature. Moreover, other than the important message which James carried and which had to be discussed at the proper place, they both assumed that whatever there was to be talked about was common knowledge to them both.

James's house had changed much with the transition from government office . . .to a place of rest from employment. The pressure lamp had been replaced by a more economical kerosene lantern and there was a little more order in the sitting room. The dust on the books had been wiped off either because of use or because of a new sense of order inflicted by Teresa.

The two men sat down solemnly on either side with their elbows on the table much like two chiefs negotiating an armistice. Teresa walked in with an aluminium kettle of milk-tea smelling heavily of cinnamon. She too said nothing as she handed the two men wooden mugs full of the yellow liquid. She poured some for herself into a broken porcelain cup. She sat down on a stool next to the wall inside James's shadow, and kept rotating the cup in her lap either because the milk-tea was too hot or because she felt the occasion too serious.

The men sipped their tea without exchanging a word for some time. Then finally James broke the silence. 'Baranya, I've got a job.'

'That's very nice to hear: What kind of a job?' Ntanya said without much feeling. Is this all he called me for he was thinking with anger in his thoughts. Try as he might, he failed to visualise his last employer taking him again and yet here was James, who had hardly been out of a job a few weeks, back in another.

He was almost feeling the same way as when he had been outside that same door, when James interrupted saying, 'I've been working as a tax collector for Kachawanga for the last four days. It's not been easy.' 'He pointed to a round copper-coated emblem stuck on the left pocket of a brown khaki uniform hanging on the wall.' As soon as people see my badge the men either disappear into their huts or start talking to their wives as if they were visitors from some distant village. What bothers me most, however, is the hostile look in the children's

110

eyes as they cling to their mothers' legs and clothes with their protruding kwashiakwor balloons of stomachs. It was as if I was responsible for their empty stomachs and at the same time as if I was a wild animal to be eaten. Anyway that's not what I called you here for. You've got enough of your own children pointing at empty stomachs.'

Teresa who had not so much as shifted the kanga on her head, came to refill James's mug and warm up Ntanya's. Without saying a word she went back to her position, and moved her chair out from James's shadow.

After taking a couple of quick sips of the tea and blowing air through his mouth to cool the burnt tip of his tongue, James continued, 'Teresa told me all, Baranya. It's a difficult situation. I may be wrong, but you've never been too good at practical things, rather like me, I suppose. That's why I think Teresa will be so good for you. At any rate she is only a woman and though she might be an exception one can't afford to take a woman's advice too seriously. I think you can and must take mine seriously. At your father's grave you asked me to stand by you. This is all I am asking to do. I agree that you cannot have Teresa cultivate your own plot and therefore I've arranged that two teams of cattle will cultivate the eastern part of my plot and that will be for your household. Not only will their cultivation be done by cattle-paid labourers unrelated to you, but we'll make it look as if you bought the land from me after cultivation for a year's service.' There was silence except for the clanking of the iron roof in the wind and echoes of children playing merrily a few households to the north. Ntanya drank his tea without registering any feelings on his face. Teresa came and with one hand holding the kettle and the other on Ntanya's back filled his mug with the now none too hot cinnamon milk-tea. After finishing his second cup Ntanya griped James's hand in a firm handshake, looked at Teresa without a smile and quietly walked back home.

James had not expected a verbal statement from Ntanya.

After looking for some time at the empty space where Ntanya had been a little earlier he went back to the desk and started counting the day's collection. Teresa said goodnight and went to James's mother's hut to sleep. As she cleared the litter of pots and gourds to make room for the cow-hide on which she was going to sleep, there was great joy in her heart which made her sing quietly in her region of non-words. Softly she hummed in the darkness after extinguishing the tin paraffin burner, interrupting it only here and there to brush off the cockroaches or other insects crawling on her. Softly, she hummed herself to sleep and dreamed of her happiness tree.

There was happiness too in Onya's heart as she checked for the third time on the following day that Ntanya had stopped Teresa hoeing.

A great many days mingled into each other, slowly and imperceptibly. Bright and some not so bright sunrises had paled into sunset again and again with a tiring repetition that no one noticed. Unnoticed, this repetition brought back normality into Ntanya's household as the grim veil of mourning was slowly turned on its back, first by the children who for some time had had to reserve their merry-making, for reasons they could understand, until they could get out of sight of the elders. This they had done quite often even though it meant dashing out under the pretext of going to relieve themselves every other hour or so. Slowly the children started to laugh watchfully. Getting no reproachful look from the elders they laughed more boisterously as they started playing with their grandmother. It could not be said that the children missed their father. It really could not be said that anybody missed him. As the days passed a new gloss appeared on everybody's faces. Without doubt everybody but Ntanya had brought from deep under their skins a new richer colour as if the death of the father and that mourning, though ambiguous, had cleansed them deep underneath. Even the old soul came out of the mourning with a loose shining skin that contrasted with the deep furrows on her face. Her mood also was complementary to this internal conflict, being at once gay and tragic. It was gay when she sat in the sun, which she did all day even when the newly hatched chicks themselves slept under the blanket beneath the banana trees, or when she blindly extended her limbs into the evening-meal fire, invariably poking her fingers and toes right into the flames till she had to be pulled off, streaked with the black of wood charcoal and ashes. It was gay when she would swallow unchewed big chunks of fire-hot meat and banana stew sighing with satisfaction as she felt the balls rolling down and the heat settling down in her stomach. It was tragic when she paused in between her loud monologues with her dead husband, son and relatives, before yelling to them, cursing them, for not responding to her conversation. Sometimes, if she happened to be talking to a dead woman relative, Onya would mimic her and then the mother would chuckle in satisfaction and go to sleep with a twisted smile. The family seemed to have accepted her old age delirium as it did not interfere at all with their newly discovered life.

Only Ntanya remained apart from this rejuvenation. In fact, far from a new hope showing on his skin, he had become thinner and his skin had acquired an ashy coarseness. Three perpendicular furrows were starting to fold on his face between the eyebrows, in keeping, probably, with his dignified role of head of the family. It could be that he was getting thinner due to his not eating well, much to the disappointment of Onya. But it could also be due to a new aloof moroseness which played on his face. When the mourning ended he had started working heavily all day, building fences around the land to be cultivated, helping Onya to hoe, making granaries for the next season. All the time he would not say a word to anybody. He would then come back to the family after work was over, and stare at the fire while holding his younger brother in his lap till food would be ready. Then he would go to sleep without saying a word, communicating, if he had to, in lethargic signals and gestures. This had gone on even through the planting season. When this was over he would go to visit Teresa and James, much to the joy of the children, for they had started to see in him a replica of their father, since moroseness has a way of spreading itself like a contagious disease. When at James's, he would sit down knitting his fingers or playing with this or that in his hands. He would ignore the fretting of Teresa about such things as his eating habits and what was to happen tomorrow. He would leave James nervous or wondering why he even went there at all.

In the meantime, the long-awaited great rains had set in for days on end. It was just as if someone had punched small holes in the bottom of the great blue sea above.

Some sort of magnanimous person, so as not to frighten Kachawanga, had covered these holes with black clouds. It poured and poured in spastic thrusts, punctuated by deafening thunder and by lightning. Once in a while it would stop with the same breathless violence, only to gather speed and pour again. The whole land and the dusty earth received this downpour with a sigh of relief and open hands, the tree branches bending down to take their long-awaited bath and the brown earth greedily soaking up the water. At the beginning, the children forgot about their play and stared bright-eyed from half-open doors and cracks at the miracle of the rain, whispering to each other 'Isn't it wonderful?' As days passed they got used to it and started playing in it naked, hurling big messy blocks of mud at each other and crying and swearing in their innocent fury and pain as the black-brown putty found its way in to their eyes. It was on one such occasion that Onya, tired of being bounced between the half-intelligible chatter of her granny and the heavy moroseness of her brother, walked out into the pouring clean rain to separate the fighting children. Apparently Moita, the youngest of the children had hurled a ball of mud right in the eyes of a boy and in revenge the boy had covered her face with this black-brown cream. They had started a fight. He stuck mud into her mouth, nose and eyes. She hit him ineffectively in the stomach. Onya stood there with her arms akimbo and the rain dripping down her neck and back as if she was looking at a cocks' fight and wanted to let them have it out. Finally she gave an order to the older children, which was immediately obeyed, to take Moita and wash her, indicating clear water filling a broken pot a few steps away.

She then bent down herself and picked a handful of mud, squashed it into her mouth and let it drip back to the ground, all the time looking way out to the western hills which could not be completely seen through the rain. She was completely unaware of being drenched and of her clothing sticking to her indecently. She could see the earth all around her starting to heave with a new life and, as the rain took a break, leaving behind cool pungent air, she could see across the village all the way to the western hills a new colour, a new year, a new life. Instead of the ashy brown of a few weeks before there was a glossy, though still unsteady, greenness all over the earth. She suddenly wanted to see whether the maize seeds she had planted had germinated and so she walked down to check. On her way to her cultivated plot she passed by her father's grave and here two green weeds were struggling up. She picked one, held it in her hand much like a person picking a rose, and walked on. Her maize seeds indeed had come up though they had not unfolded their secret in leaves yet. She knelt down with her knees deep in the mud and pulled out one and held it in the hand in which she was holding the weed from her father's grave. Looking at them and noticing that their glossy green and yellow colour was all smeared with the mud in her hand she opened her hand and let them drop back to the wet earth. As she did so a great agitation seemed to be growing inside her. Holding first her breast and then her stomach a great desire came into her. She felt, as she looked at the now black earth bringing forth life, that she was being cheated, cheated very badly. The future with Ntanya in his present condition showed no improvement day after day. It gave no hope for her future either. 'I'll run away,' she said fiercely to herself. 'I'll run away, to any place. To the town maybe and look for work, any work and maybe if I clean myself a little and learn Swahili better I might be able to get an educated husband who will give me children, children, children,' she yelled with her fists clenched and shaking. One could not tell whether the stream of clear liquid dripping down her cheeks was her tears or the rain.

When Onya got home, her grandmother was saying, in agitation more shrill and more interrupted than usual, repeating again and again 'I won't live through this.'

Ntanya was not at home. He must have left for James's. The children, reconciled by then, were playing noisily at the southern end of the hut, unaware of the aged mother. As soon as Onya heard this she lost the moony listlessness of the field. She knelt by the old soul, put more wood on the fire and covered herself up properly. She said, 'No mother, you've lived through so many other rainy seasons you'll also live through this one.'

The old woman did not reply; maybe she did not hear; it could also have been that she ignored Onya because she did not believe her. Onya felt a great weight of guilt on her chest at how she could have even thought of deserting the family; her sense of guilt was reflected in the quantity and quality of that day's supper. As she was laying herself down to sleep that night, exhausted in more than one way, she swore silently and bitterly to herself a holy oath (for all oaths taken by oneself to oneself are holy) that she would never leave ths family not even if she had a man to run to. She tried to convince herself, but only half-successfully, that those children who had been playing noisily while their grandmother had been saying that she was not going to last were in fact her own. She was only half successful because the desire nudging in her was still shaking its head in disagreement and because, just before she was relieved by sleep, a new fear was silently speaking to her as she realised that she probably needed her grandmother more than the grandmother needed her. As it was she still had parents in her grandmother; if the old one died she would then be completely disowned, and all the humiliation of her being an orphan would be complete. As if she had turned into a child and as if she was afraid of the booming thunder outside she moved quietly in the dark to her grandmother's bed and putting her hand on her grandmother's bony shoulder went to sleep nudging close to her.

When Ntanya had got to James's place that violent late afternoon he found Teresa sitting alone on the threshold with her legs crossed, but level to the ground, most of them sticking out into the rain. She was absent-mindedly knitting and unknitting the same strand of banana-leaf basket without making any progress. She was in great agitation, trembling from time to time much as she had been the day she had first met Ntanya at Maria's. She did not as much as move to let Ntanya in, and he had to squeeze himself in out of the rain. James was not in.

Ntanya sat at the table, knitting his fingers in the same futile way as Teresa was knitting the banana leaves, opening and closing his mouth, not knowing what to say or how to say it. Teresa seemed to have a peculiar type of command over Ntanya for, even during the time when he had been moving from his house to James's in a reverie he would dream on. Only, when

Teresa started talking or laughing then Ntanya would find his way through back again to the world of reality. There was a way in which Teresa's moods and presence spread themselves. There was restlessness all around the room and both wanted to say something but neither did. Finally Teresa threw the unfinished basket into the rain and walked over to Ntanya. She stood in between his legs without smiling or touching him. She looked at him for some time and then with her hand on his knee turned around to face the rain. With her eyes fixed on the threshold, she asked Ntanya loudly, as if she was addressing a meeting, 'What is going to happen to us?'

Ntanya, fully jolted from his weeks-old dream, did not understand what she meant, and even after she had repeated herself he said, 'Oh, I don't know. Same thing that happens to everybody else, I guess.' It was not a reply but only as a registration of his presence. Feeling a little guilty he said, 'We'll get married soon.'

Teresa turned to face him. There was no joy in her face. In fact tears were collecting on her eyelids. 'I didn't mean that,' she said drawling her words with pain.

'Then what did you mean?'

'I don't know. I don't know how to express it. Maybe you won't understand. It's just that I'd expected life with you. Now it seems as if all I'm going to get is the death-life of Maria's house,' she said flinging herself from him and going back to the threshold. It seemed as if getting these words out relieved her, her face became calmer.

'I don't understand what you mean,' Ntanya said, as he moved and sat next to her on the threshold with his hand on her neck. She did not resist his touch. 'I've never been too good at understanding other people, I suppose even at understanding myself. But . . .'

Teresa interrupted. 'What's happening to you Ntanya? Why do you have to destroy yourself and us and blame other people for it? Your father died, many people's fathers have died. You've
118

lost a job, think you are a bastard, and so on and so on. All these things and more have happened to other people. They have not gone around destroying other people's lives because of it! Why, you've never had a man rip off your clothes and make love to you on a cold cement floor and then stick money in your mouth.' She put her face on his chest and her tears dripped down his stomach as she continued very softly. 'I've been waiting, Ntanya darling. Every day after I come back from the fields I've been waiting for you to come out of whatever is eating you. I've been waiting for you to say one nice thing to me, or say you love me or need me. It was easy when I was at Maria's house. I could carry on and on that life-death because that's all I had known. But then you came along and taught me to care, taught me to love and we walked. Many days have gone by, and the maize I planted is now touching my waist, and all you do is move around like a ghost. Please don't destroy me, please!'

Ntanya did not reply for some time. He just held her close to him. Tears were still streaming from her eyes but she was quite calm. Finally Ntanya said softly 'I didn't know. My God I didn't know. My God I didn't know. It all sounds very futile sometimes, this attempt to differentiate between dream and reality. You know I do love you more than anything Teresa; but somehow when a man has an itch on his back he drops the spoon he is eating with to scratch his back. Only I've been stretching my arm to scratch my itch and I can't pinpoint the itching point. Maybe I never will be able to.'

'Then let me scratch your back for you,' Teresa said as she stroked his back.

'Sometimes I think, no matter what we do, we're bound to destroy each other some day. I don't mean only you and me, I mean all human relations. All human relations seem to me to lead directly, somehow or another, to destruction as sure as life leads to death. Because we have this seed of destruction in us we spread it, much like a disease. My father, for instance, picked it up somewhere and spread it to me and I to you and so on. This is why I've been looking so carefully in the dream-world of my history to see whether I could pluck out this thread of sickness for your own sake and mine and the children to come. It's not my being a bastard or poor that has been bothering me. It's something much deeper, much much deeper! Something at my very foundation that has caused all these symptoms. You are quite right, many people have suffered worse happenings than these. Some have just got used to them, others relieved themselves of this awareness in the various forms of life-death that you are only too aware of. Others, I am sure, have hit their heads against the tough hard wall like myself and decided like I am deciding right now – to throw themselves head first into the dirty pool of life that they can't clean.'

Teresa did not understand what Ntanya was talking about; maybe Ntanya did not understand what he was talking about either. Although she did not understand what Ntanya was talking about she fully understood the new vigour in Ntanya's embraces and, looking up to him like a child responding to a sugar-banana that it has been crying for, Teresa straightened herself up, and like a little child rubbed dry her tears on her eyes and Ntanya's chest. Teresa was about to say something, and from the way her lips were parted it must have been an endearment, when James and Mary walked in. He had a large basket on his shoulder.

'Don't let me bother you,' he said, 'I'm going to have my own soon too.'

'Really Baranya, who, who?' Teresa said jumping up and relieving James of the heavy basket.

'No hurry, you'll know in time,' James said. He had been drinking and he looked merrier than he had been before. 'Baranya,' he said with his hand on Ntanya's shoulder, 'You've got to be happy for me today. You absolutely have to, that's an order.' Wiggling a finger at him like a pedagogue emphasising a point and doing a little dance in short rather silly steps he went on in his half-drunken voice. 'I'm so happy today. If you don't become happy with me I'll wring off your head,' he said twisting Ntanya's strong neck ineffectively. 'Why, let us celebrate the independence of Yakampath with that basket. I think it is today isn't it?'

Neither Ntanya nor Teresa had heard of the exotic name before, but in between their laughter they both said, 'Yes' and, looking at each other, they laughed even harder. They laughed on and on till tears were streaming out of Ntanya's eyes, laughed for this strange country whose independence they were about to celebrate and laughed for the world and the green maize plants that were growing so fast. But most of all they laughed at their newly unearthed happiness, unearthed from so deep down in the mud of living. Ntanya, most of all, seemed as if he had saved all his laughter for a long time, and as he gasped for breath Teresa moved over to him, afraid that he would choke, but though he would stop when their eyes met, he went on laughing in periodic spurts. Finally, when Ntanya stopped with a broad grin on his face the three folds between his eyebrows had disappeared. Teresa walked over to him and whispered, 'We don't have to destroy each other, darling.' Ntanya stood up laughing, hardly finishing the sentence, 'Damn right we don't have to. Open the beer.'

They started drinking to the health of Yakampath. 'Now Baranya,' Ntanya said after finishing a bottle, 'Seriously, what are you celebrating? Have you had a salary rise? You couldn't be celebrating this country's independence, surely.'

'Why I could even be celebrating my being a man. Why, if I was a woman I'd have five little bastards now,' James said, with his tongue playing with the beer in the glass. He was a bit drunk.

'Yes, you certainly would have.' They all laughed.

James then maintained a soberish seriousness, though one could still see a smile sneaking in at the corners of his mouth as he started, 'No, Baranya, I have just met on my tax-collecting rounds today an old woman, a widow with her legs swollen with elephantiasis and her one eye completely blind. She invited me to share her maize in groundnuts for lunch. You know I've never seen more life before. She was bubbling with happiness about how simply grand it was to be living, and she could not even move. She opened my eyes to the life and joy in me which has been wasted so much. I promised her a regular portion of my salary every month. Why she has really saved me. There is so much, so much to live for. Why Baranya, how much we have wasted of ourselves complaining incessantly about trivialities just like a bunch of fertile women who are reluctant to go to bed with men, complaining about being childless, while that old woman has had everything simply because she has nothing. But you know I've made up my mind that I'm going to go to bed and get pregnant and raise that child if it kills me and that is what I am celebrating.' They all laughed again. This time they were all warmed up by the beer. They drank on and on until James was totally drunk.

Finally Ntanya got up and said, 'I too have made up my mind that I'm going to bed. But I'm not going to get pregnant, somebody else is going to,' he said, winking at Teresa. She smiled but in her shyness she looked down.

'Why don't you sleep here today?' James said starting to move towards his bed.

'Be-ca-u-se if I sleep here tonight, warmed up as I am, somebody will suffer. Goodnight and long live Yawa whatever it is.' He disappeared into the darkness.

Teresa jerked herself up to see him disappear into the darkness. As he disappeared he seemed to be walking right into her heart, filling it up. 'Goodnight my love, do be careful,' she said into the darkness as she walked over into the women's hearth hut to sleep and dream.

That year they harvested a bumper crop. Everywhere green-yellow plants would be seen sighing in the wind under the pleasant load of the cobs which, as Onya once said to herself silently looking at the giant plants were 'as long as one's thigh.' The banana trees too were bent down close to the earth by bunches, green and full. And the cassava, sweet potatoes and yams were cracking broad crevices on the face of the earth. Everywhere around Kachawanga there was joy, hidden silent joy in mothers' and fathers' hearts, hidden because one is never sure of a harvest till one has pulled it all into the storage bins. There could be an invasion of locusts or strange birds before harvesting. There could even be disease, to balance such a phenomenal crop.

The children expressed their joys outwardly. There was a new green-maize gloss on their faces and their play and quarrels echoed again and again off little round stomachs full of boiled maize and bananas. Like squirrels gnawing a dry monkey-nut, the children ate the maize continuously, boiled or grilled on paraffin tin containers or even cooked in leaves on their unsteady fires; and when they got tired of eating they would chew it, make balls of it and fight with them. The children would then go home in the evening with tired grins of satisfaction and fall down on their mothers' laps saying, 'Mother, give me water.' And then the mothers would smile with great satisfaction, for in Kachawanga there is nothing that creates more joy in a mother than the sight of a round full stomach on her children. They would give their children cold curdled milk from full black-brown gourds and then the children would sleep with their grins changed into smiles. The nights were therefore quiet in Kachawanga, since the children did not play. In this stillness fear and joy constantly exchanged places in the hearts of the adults. Some would even imagine a zooming noise of brown northern locusts. They could visualise the empty stalks pointing with despair to the heavens. They waited and waited in uneasiness looking to the north for a brown cloud, but nothing came up from the north. They waited for a foul wind from the east but there was nothing but calmness all over the land. All over Kachawanga one would see crowds talking unhurriedly for, while waiting for the reaping season, there was not much to do, someone throwing a look quickly to the east or the north as if they were anticipating somebody they were telling stories about. As the maize started growing brown and the chances of a locust-swarm seemed remoter with each passing day, adults too started comparing the thickness of the bananas and fruits and maize cobs, each one saying 'But mine is bigger,' and laughing about their gone-by fears.

This mixture of joy and fear had also been in Ntanya's heart. But since he had been so busy building his wedding hut he had not had time to think much about it. Now as he was putting the fine-ash mud finish on the outside walls of the hut the joyous part of his feelings started to express itself more and more. He had reason to be even happier than most people in Kachawanga as he went into daydreams, with a big cob of boiled maize in his hands, about the good things hidden in his coming marriage. He had by now forgotten all about his father, save on a few occasions when he had passed by his father's green grave; even his memories excited only remote and mellow feelings. Onya too was a source of great joy for him after James and she had become engaged.

One day however, as Teresa and Ntanya were decorating the thatched roof of the hut, he remembered his father with strong feelings. Teresa had been talking about how that morning she had noticed for the first time a maize plant that had four cobs on it. Ntanya became lost in thought for a while, and then said 'It's strange isn't it; that my father dies and then we get the best harvest for generations in Kachawanga?'

'You must not think that way Ntanya,' Teresa said. 'There is no relationship between the death of your father and this year's good harvest.'

Ntanya was not listening. He went on 'Even the twig planted on his grave has grown. It has already flowered.'

'What do you mean? Why shouldn't it grow?' Teresa was disturbed.

'I don't know. Pass me the knife.'
They did not mention the subject again.

The wedding was quiet. After harvests, weddings and mournings are always quiet in Kachawanga, largely because, since every household has got sufficient food, nobody cares to walk for the free meat, maize meal and millet beer which they have got galore in their own households. There were therefore only about two dozen people at Ntanya's wedding. Neither the bride nor the bridegroom minded this much, since this meant that they could be left alone earlier. A little emptiness was felt however during the bride presentation dance since Teresa's relatives had to be represented by five or so of Ntanya's friends. It was only at this point that a little sorrow was seen to play on Teresa's face. Ntanya too had a little sadness in his heart as he looked over to his grandmother's stool and noticed that Miila's wife was sitting there to represent his grandmother who had died in her sleep a few weeks before. Her death had not come as a shock to anybody and nobody mourned her since she had lived every bit of her life out till she had reached a point where there was nothing else to live. All over Kachawanga people had only sighed on hearing of her death saying that she was a lucky and sinless woman to have been able to wear out even her gums. Even her own grandchildren had not cried. They had just buried her facing west to signify a duly concluded life, much as one removes a flaking on a scar and forgets about it. All the same, as Ntanya looked at her stool he missed her and wished she was there, just there in person, even to complain about the sun's heat again.

As the evening drew near the visitors went, leaving behind presents of sheep, goats, chickens, even a cow and best wishes would do from now on.

Teresa had not felt quite so easy. She knew that Ntanya there for the first time and for many more days to come. With this new home a great feeling of freshness surged in Ntanya. It was indeed a beginning. Everything depended on what they would do from now on.

Teresa had not felt quite so easy. She knew that Ntanya knew that she was not a virgin, and furthermore she also knew that since she had no relatives Ntanya could not demand on the following morning, a goat as a fine for her not being a virgin, but she felt uneasy all the same. Even when yielding to him she was afraid that she might not satisfy him, but her hesitation was nullified by Ntanya's controlled violence. When they finally came together she cried out from the depth of her being 'It is beautiful, it is beautiful, life is so beautiful.' And it was true, life as she saw it then was beautiful. The world presented itself to her closed eyes in a multi-coloured panorama circulating, teasing and dancing before her like dancers cajoling before a chief. It was beautiful, and she could never forget that phrase all that night. Ntanya, for his part, was repeating to himself over and over again 'Yes we have made a good start.' Teresa did not feel like washing herself all over the way she had felt at Maria's house, and there was no sour taste in the back of Ntanya's mouth as he peacefully went to sleep.

Days passed full of all kinds of joys. At first they came together quite often but the habit soon wore out, and soon they found their joys in just being together, working, eating together quite often but the habit soon wore out, and soon When Ntanya looked bored she would come over and make passes at him saying, 'Well, you didn't think that I could wear you out, did you?' And then Ntanya would laugh and chase her just like a little boy.

Soon there was Onya's marriage to James and this too was

a source of great joy for both of them, especially for Teresa who delighted in taking care of the children on her own.

Days passed fast for Ntanya and Teresa. They could hardly notice the land getting brown all over Kachawanga again, since neither of them hardly noticed any more the sun come up and go down. Ntanya would work very hard in the field hauling in the last harvest and Teresa would stay at home washing, cooking and waiting, waiting for him to come home. She would cook his meal with extra care and when there was little meat she would only give bits to the children and not even touch it herself but use only the smell to get her food down and reserve the whole chunk for her husband. When Ntanya would come home with sweat on his brows she would put the wooden tray on a stool for him and sit down by him watching him eat with great satisfaction; every bolus that went down Ntanya's throat would also go down her own throat. When Ntanya would insist on sharing the food with her she would always say she had eaten already no matter how hungry she might be. Ntanya would then eat and drink to his satisfaction and always rest for a while in the sun after saying 'Thank you mother.'

When Ntanya came home one day he noticed that Teresa was even happier than usual. It could not have been merely because James had been promoted and he and Onya were therefore going to live in the big town that Onya had dreamt so much about. It could not even have been because James had left a farewell parcel for Ntanya with a new pair of trousers and a shirt in it. No, she was happy because of something else, and Ntanya knew it. This was Ntanya's time to feel the way Teresa had felt when she'd sat down patiently watching the good food she had cooked go down his throat. He felt as if what was happening in Teresa was happening in his own body and this made him almost stand on his toes and shout. But what was happening was so deep down inside him that he could never shout out loud enough to get it out. Instead he walked over to her and gripping her head tight in his sweating hands said softly, 'My darling you have saved me, you have vindicated me. Now I am fulfilled, now I have possessed in my hands that which I could not understand.' Teresa raised her eyes to him. She did not say anything. There was nothing to be said. Tears were rolling out of her eyes and she looked down again as Ntanya released her head and walked west to nowhere towards the setting sun.

Ntanya watched Teresa's belly grow bigger and bigger each day, each week. Every day he would sneak a shy look at this rounding of her belly, this fullness emanating out of the seed of their happiness like a child checking again and again whether the bean he planted in a tin was growing. Teresa thought he was watching and she too sneaked a shy look at him to check whether he actually was. Then their eyes would meet, they understood and only laughed. And every day Ntanya would water this seed with his joy, with this vigilance and care.

Finally the baby was born. It was a boy. Ntanya called it Nterenya after his father and nicknamed it 'The Avenger'. They took care of it and watched it grow the way they had watched the belly grow only with more patience. And as it grew it resembled Ntanya's father more and more. As Ntanya saw his father's image reproduced almost perfectly in The Avenger's face, eyes and ears he walked over to the forgotten grave of his father and wept bitterly, kneeling on the soft grass that had grown up, repeating 'My, father, my, my, my . . . my own true father. Pardon me, I have done you great wrong, pardon me.' When he got home Teresa was playing with The Avenger. He motioned the child to come to him but the child shook its head and ran to its mother's lap.

Ntanya laughed hysterically saying 'Life is a circle just like the middle of that pot over there.' Teresa was disturbed as she came with the baby in her arms and knelt by him asking what he meant. He smoothed the soft earth of the hut's floor and with one hand on her shoulder said 'Look at my finger, I start here.' He drew an almost perfect circle on the brown soft earth. 'I end here exactly where I started. That is life.' They went on laughing. Teresa did not understand, but The Avenger was sleeping so she went to put him to bed.

> *Thy firmness draws my circle just*
> *And makes me end where I began.*

PR
9898
T3v
P154
D9

Palangyo, Peter K 1939–
    Dying in the sun ₁by₁ Peter K. Palangyo.   London,
Heinemann Educational, 1969.
    ₍5₎, 129 p.   19 cm.   (African writers series, 53)   8/–   ($1.25)
                                                        B 69–27270

    Label mounted on t. p.: New York, Humanities Press.

    ₁. Title.   II. Series.

226713   PZ4.P1546Dy 3   823   70 ₍2₎
        [PR9066.A4]
        SBN 435–90053–6

    Library of Congress